MW00908601

HOSPITAL HILL

KATHERINE ANDERSON

For Bruce who tolerates my increasing addiction to the written word.

This book exists because of you.

To my parents who didn't even know this novel existed but voted for it anyway.

Published by Makin Books LLC

Copyright ©2016 Katherine Anderson

All rights reserved.

No part of this book may be reproduced in any form, except for the inclusion of brief quotations in review, without permission in writing from the author/publisher.

While every precaution has been taken in the preparation of this book, the publisher assumes no responsibility for errors or omissions, or for damages resulting from the information contained herein.

NOTE FROM THE AUTHOR:

We greatly appreciate you taking the time to read our work. Please consider leaving a review wherever you bought the book, or telling your friends about this book to help us spread the word. Thank you so much for your support.

FOREWORD

Northampton State Hospital was the first abandoned state hospital I ever explored on a cold winter day in 2002. At the time I was working at a residential treatment facility in Western Massachusetts that I found had historical ties to the state hospital system. I can still remember the first time I saw Hospital Hill, driving up Route 66 and seeing the Gothic giant looming out of the trees like something out of a horror film, a stone castle that sprawled across acres upon acres of land, completely abandoned and surrounded by chain link. It was by far one of the most beautiful buildings I had ever seen.

After doing a bit of online research I learned that Northampton was just one of many asylums across the nation built on the same architectural plan designed by Dr. Thomas Kirkbride of Pennsylvania. I began traveling all over New England visiting and photographing as many asylums as I possibly could, painstakingly researching each location as I went. By 2006 I had assembled enough information to self-publish my first nonfiction compilation of asylum history.

However, Northampton remained my first love and I continued to read all the available history, attending meetings of the Memorial Committee, and finally, in 2013, photographed the moving of the Memorial Complex cupola from storage to its new home at Commonwealth Academy. I began toying with the idea of writing a novel about Northampton after having read a number of wonderful asylum based stories, but I wasn't certain how to bring the hospital to life. The greatest challenge in creating the fictional Hospital

Hill, was creating fictional characters who would do justice to the real Northampton State Hospital. Hopefully I have managed to do this, and do it well.

As you read Hospital Hill, I encourage any and all comments, suggestions, corrections, and anecdotes. Over the years I have enjoyed hearing from my readers who frequently include former staff members, mental health workers, and occasionally former patients. I also encourage you to follow me on social media, including Goodreads and Amazon's WriteOn where you will get a sneak peek at the coming prequel/sequel to Hospital Hill.

For more information and suggested readings on asylum history, visit www.asylumaveartists.com.

Kate
@PoisonedPenner
katherine.anderson415@gmail.com

CHAPTER 1

Valerie Martin's last day at Westborough State Hospital was uneventful. Everyone in her department knew that she didn't like fanfare so instead of the usual niceties of cake and a public send off, someone circulated a card and left it on her desk along with an empty file box. That was on Thursday. On Friday she purposefully chose an early morning train from Worcester in order to avoid the commuters, arriving to find the Springfield station quiet under the dingy yellow of the fluorescent lights over the ticket booths.

"Excuse me," she said, reaching out to grab a passing porter, but withdrawing her hand just shy of his sleeve. "Can I still get a cab from here?"

"Yes ma'am." He nodded, gesturing toward the escalator inside the station. "Take that down to the street. There should be a few waiting."

As her cab crested the hill on Route 66 Val caught her first glimpse of Hospital Hill—the looney bin, the bug house—Northampton State Hospital. Though it was nearing dusk and there were no lights left burning on the now abandoned campus, Valerie could envision exactly what waited, crouched in grayscale behind chain link fences; the buildings that were now being readied for demolition, the buildings that had once been alive, brightly lit, and filled with the hustle of daily routines-- the heart of the hill.

It had been nearly fifteen years since she left Northampton for Westborough and she wasn't quite certain how she felt about her return. Though on one hand it had been simple to leave Westborough as she wasn't married and had no family to speak of, it had still been an emotionally draining decision. She had been so close to retiring from the Department of Mental Health but she had had a difficult time saying no, pushing aside that light at the end of the tunnel she had been dreaming of—a tiny house somewhere at the top of a hill, preferably not around the corner from a hospital.

Valerie had spent the bulk of her career at the Northampton State Hospital for the Insane, but in the spring of 1980, after the first major wave of patients had been released from the dying shadow of an asylum, she had seen the proverbial writing on the wall and taken advantage of the department's offer to relocate her. She headed out to Westborough and hadn't looked back—until her former colleague Bill Dunston had called. He had sounded rather reluctant on the phone, but he said the department was desperate. They needed for a former NSH staff member to assemble patient reports in the Haskell Building, a task that would likely take a few months to complete and the department had specifically requested Valerie. Though she couldn't necessarily say she was pleased with the idea of coming back to Western Massachusetts, Westborough was now preparing for closure as well, so she agreed to one final, rather menial task, but one she knew she could accomplish with her eyes closed.

Retrieving her suitcase from the trunk of the cab, Valerie hitched her purse onto her shoulder. She glanced at her watch to find that it was 11:50 and she was due to meet Bill at noon, which meant she would have to take the battered and rather aged case with her. While the rest of the campus crumbled around it, the Haskell Building, the last operating DMH building, hadn't changed a bit. It was a squat, two-story C-shaped building and though it was constructed of brick like the rest of the campus, it had been added in the 1950's so it was not nearly as ornate or well built. The rows of windows cut into the facade were horizontal rectangles that tilted out, making it look as if the building was winking at passersby. Valerie pushed through the front door and headed for the basement where the records rooms were, and where Bill Dunston kept his office.

"Bill?" She knocked tentatively, hesitant to find how he might receive her.

"Valerie. Welcome back." Bill said, the pleasantry ringing false to Valerie's ears. He pulled himself up from behind his desk, and Valerie was shocked at how he had changed, yet somehow looked so much the same. He was still painfully skinny, still tall and gangly, all arms and legs, but he had grown a paunch and there were bags under his eyes, his hair thinned a great deal. He pushed his wire-rimmed glasses up onto the bridge of his nose and fairly glared at Valerie with what could have been indifference but bordered on open resentment.

Catching sight of her suitcase, Bill turned to his desk and grabbed an envelope. "You can put your bag down if you like while I show you around. This is everything you need for your housing," he said, handing her the envelope. "The hospital still owns that white cottage around the corner, right next to the chapel."

Nodding, Valerie tucked the envelope into her purse and stowed her suitcase next to Bill's desk.

"So, you ready to dive in?"

"Absolutely."

"Alright. Follow me." Bill grabbed a set of keys off his desk and led Valerie out into the hallway and down to the last records room on the right. "This is the block of patient records you'll be working with. I called you for the job because these date from 1960 to 1979 so most of these patients you'll recognize, same with the docs and ward designations. The majority of that coding changed after you left in the eighties so any kind of reporting by a more recent employee would have been meaningless."

Unlocking the door, Bill ushered Valerie into the cavernous room and gestured at the walls of file cabinets. "Now, all we need to do is track some simple population data that will be turned over to the Department of Mental Health. They want to know how many males, how many females, how many of each diagnosis, meds, ward assignments...oh and how many patients to each doc. And it all needs to be classified by year. Obviously these are all arranged alphabetically so each file has to be gone through individually. It's a logistical nightmare."

Bill finally stopped talking, much to Valerie's relief, and took note of her raised eyebrows. He had to realize it was a ridiculous task that had no bearing on the remaining hospital operations but it was, unfortunately, a Department request. Valerie could handle it easily, but that didn't stop her from silently kicking herself for picking up Bill's call in the first place.

"Now, I promised you lunch so why don't we head upstairs and I can answer any questions you might have."

In spite of Bill's breezy tone, Valerie sensed he was uncomfortable with her being there. Perhaps he too was kicking himself for having brought her back. Thirty years ago when he transferred in from Taunton State Hospital, two years into Valerie's stint on the wards, the strain on their relationship had developed almost immediately. There was an eight year age difference between them and though Bill was older, he was stubborn and emotionally stunted. Which wasn't to say he wasn't good at his job, because he was, he was just something of a petulant brat with an inability to see sense when it came to Valerie.

They sat together at a table, both reluctant to be the first to break the uneasy silence. Eating gave them something to do but eventually one of them would be faced with an empty plate.

"Who am I reporting to for this whole mess?" Valerie kept her eyes on her plate, pushing her salad around with her fork.

"To be honest, no one really. You're essentially on your own. The department just used me to get you here."

There was no surprise in that. This seemed to be one of those projects that would be completed only to be tossed in the circular file once it made its way to Boston. "Is there a particular form I should be using or anything I should know before I start?"

Bill snickered. "Of course there are forms, but for now just organize it however you see fit. The information will be compiled and beaten into shape later." He cleared his throat and put down his fork. "So I assume you know Robert Willard passed a few years ago."

Valerie flinched, then nodded. "Yes, I heard. Accident of some kind?"

"A nasty fall down the stairs in his home. His ex-wife-- you remember Julia I'm sure- well, she found him. Hadn't heard from him in a few days apparently, got worried. There he was on the floor. Neck broken." Bill shook his head in what Valerie knew to be more disgust than sympathy. "What a way to go."

"Yes. Though I suppose he got what he deserved, eh Bill?"

Bill chuckled then looked up to see whether Valerie was kidding him. "Indeed he did."

Valerie shook her head, equally disgusted by Bill's naked hatred of the man, even in the shadow of his death.

"I suppose I'll see you tomorrow morning." She pushed in her chair and grabbed her tray, leaving Bill in the silence of the empty cafeteria. Valerie knew that Bill had had a thing for her all those years ago, and in the end he had assumed that Valerie had fallen for the philandering Dr. Willard, just like every other red blooded female in that hospital. Though he tried to hide his disappointment, Valerie knew; knew how he had despised Robert Willard but Valerie had spent those same hears relegating Robert Willard to memory, the worst of them she found.

Suitcase in hand, Valerie walked out the front door of the Haskell Building and across the parking lot to Chapel Street, a tiny stretch of pavement tucked up on the hill beside the hospital and tried not to dwell on how soundly her meeting with Bill had failed. She pulled the envelope he had given her from her purse and fished out the keys to number 37. With any luck the movers would arrive within the hour and she would be able to settle into the little white house with the large living room and the bay window that afforded a clear view of the Haskell Building.

When the final box had been deposited in the front hallway and Valerie had closed the door on the movers, she set to work putting sheets on the bed, hung up her dresses, and refolded her blouses. She filled her bureau drawers just as they had been in her apartment in Westborough, arranged her toiletries in the bathroom, and gave the bath a quick scrub. Removing the plastic sheeting from the couch, she carried a box marked "Old" into the living room and slit the tape with a pair of scissors. She then retrieved the file box, marveling at the fact that after more than a decade at Westborough State Hospital, she had managed to rid the office of every sign of her presence in a matter of minutes while barely filling one box.

Pulling out the brass nameplate she had swiped from her desk at WSH, she added it to the pile-- her very first uniform from NSH folded neatly on top of her diploma from the Smith College School of Social Work, scattered across the bottom of the box the skeleton key from her first office at NSH and the last one at WSH that she had kept when the doors had been rekeyed.

Valerie closed the box and shoved it in the closet at the end of the hallway, then drifted into the kitchen to put the teakettle on. Holding her steaming tea in her hands, she wandered into the living room at peered out at the Haskell Building. She found herself dreading the prospect of starting again at NSH, seeing irrefutable proof that the hospital itself no longer resembled the one she remembered. Though she had only glanced at the hill on her way by in the cab, she had seen clearly how drastically it had changed. Gone was the immaculate landscaping of the manicured lawns; the white doctors' cottages were vacant and overgrown, weeds and vines tumbling all over the place, the empty windows like black eyes peering out at the main road. The buildings were cordoned off and the main gate where the staff used to wait for the bus had been removed.

Turning away from the window, Val looked around the apartment and sighed, knowing she still had quite a bit to do. She stood there for a moment and tried to clear her mind of the hospital and gave herself a pep talk of sorts. "It's just a job," she said aloud, her voice echoing back at her from the walls of the apartment. "Just a job."

On Sunday she laid out a plain navy dress and sweater, then went through her nightly routine. She took a moment to look at herself in the mirror, noting the grays creeping back into her blond again, the fine lines and wrinkles taking up residence around her eyes and mouth. When had she gotten so old? She tugged at her skin and ran her fingers through her hair, but of course she couldn't wipe away the years, so instead she switched off the bathroom light, turned in, and slept soundly until her alarm went off at 6:00 am. At 6:59 she walked into the lobby of the Haskell Building and headed down the stairs to the basement where, after a perfunctory greeting, Bill left her in the silent vacuum of the records room, surrounded by the dead, nothing left of their human spirits but a notarized death certificate and a folder full of scientific mumblings. And nothing left for Valerie but the ghosts and the nightmares—oh, the nightmares.

CHAPTER 2

It was nearly September of 1959 when Valerie Martin tucked her purse under her arm and walked the short distance up Westhampton Road to Hospital Hill where the Northampton State Hospital for the Insane perched on top like a beautiful gargoyle. Having graduated from Smith College in May, she had assumed she would find a teaching position in one of the local schools but by mid-August nothing had materialized. Though if she was being honest, she hadn't tried very hard to find something, only now her campus housing allowance was about to dry up and she knew her parents wouldn't be best pleased to learn of her lack of ambition. One afternoon as she sat at her desk reading, her roommate, Susan Tellier, suggested she apply at the asylum on the hill.

"They pay a dollar and a half an hour. That's more than any of the shops in town." Susan fluffed her hair and pulled on a lavender cardigan that perfectly matched the tiny flowers on her perfectly pressed dress. "I had an interview last week and they should be calling any day now." As she flounced out of the room, Valerie shrugged and thought, what the hell. A paycheck was a paycheck.

The hill itself was well known in town, not just because of the "looney bin" but because it was where almost everyone in town went sledding each winter. She wound her way over the road to the path that led past the doctors' houses and the wrought iron fountain to the famous portico of Old Main, the administration building, where a few cars and ambulances idled outside the doors. Valerie slipped between them through the heavy wooden doors and into the lobby where a receptionist sat guard at the foot of massive twin staircases that swept up to the floor above. Her heels clicked on the hardwood floor as she approached the woman behind the desk who was efficiently answering and transferring phone calls.

She held up a slim finger topped with a brightly polished red nail, silencing Valerie for the moment, greeting a caller with "Hello Northampton State Hospital how may I direct your call?" A moment later the woman motioned for Valerie to step forward. "Can I help you dear?"

"Valerie Martin. I'm here to apply for a position."

"Have a seat," she said, looking Valerie up and down. "I'll call Mrs. Harding for you." She gestured toward a wooden bench near the door and Valerie sat with her ankles crossed, her hands in her lap.

She had worn her favorite navy dress with the black buttons and her shoulder length blond hair was pinned away from her face which was bare of makeup. The pink flush on each of her cheeks highlighted her blue eyes set deep in her pale Irish face. As she waited she glanced around the lobby at the elegant staircase, the neatly dressed hospital staff going up and down the stairs. After waiting a good twenty minutes a woman in a smart gray skirt suit with a starched white blouse under her jacket approached Valerie. The woman who she assumed was Mrs. Harding had graying mouse-brown hair and black cat's eye glasses that framed her equally mouse-brown eyes. The only makeup she wore was her coral pink lipstick that had spread dangerously outside her lip line.

"Young lady, you'd like to apply for a position at our hospital?"

Our hospital? Valerie stood and offered her hand to the imperious looking little woman then withdrew it as she could see that Mrs. Harding had no intention of shaking it. "Yes ma'am. Valerie Martin. I just graduated from Smith College"

"And what is your degree in? Child care?"

"Well, not exactly." Valerie squared her shoulders. "Education, yes. But also English. I write."

Mrs. Harding pursed her lips and rolled her eyes ever so slightly. "Come with me. Have you ever been inside an asylum before?"

Valerie followed Mrs. Harding across the lobby to the staircase on the left. "No ma'am. I have not."

At the top of the stairs Mrs. Harding stepped aside to let a grizzle-haired woman in a gray sackcloth dress pass, a female orderly in a crisp white uniform following close behind. Mrs. Harding nodded at the orderly and reached to open a door on the right side of the hall, ushering Valerie into an office that was just as neat and fussy as the woman who occupied it.

"Now, at the moment I am in need of responsible, reliable young ladies to work on the female wing in Ward B. The duties include escorting the patients to and from activities, assisting them with their chores, and keeping them in line on the ward. You will report to the nurses who run the ward and do as they say. Does that sound like the sort of task you can handle with your fancy college degree Ms. Martin?"

Valerie snapped her head up, prepared to set Mrs. Harding straight on her views about educated women but seeing the challenging look in the woman's eyes, she simply nodded. "Yes ma'am."

"Indeed." Mrs. Harding pulled open a drawer and handed Valerie an application and a pen. "Fill out what you can. The salary is $1.50 per hour. Women don't get raises here so don't even consider it. You start next week on second shift," she said, her lips curling into a sneer. "Or will that occupy too much of your dance card?"

"No ma'am. Second shift is fine." Lord, what had she just agreed to? Valerie could feel a sudden panic taking over her earlier confidence as she turned away from Mrs. Harding, shaking her head. She wandered all the way back down the hill to her dorm where she packed the brand new blue Samsonite suitcase she had gotten for her birthday in June. Smart clothing, like her navy slacks and three white blouses went into the case along with a few pairs of sensible shoes and as many cardigans as she could fit without busting the locks. She stuffed her toiletries into the matching carry-on case along with a brand new leather journal and her fountain pen; everything else went into boxes. She called her parents to tell them the news, and though neither one reacted well when they heard the word asylum, in spite of their trepidation they agreed to pick up the rest of their daughter's things and store them.

In the basement of the main hospital, Valerie gathered her uniform from Mrs. Burke, received her lodging assignment from Mrs. Harding, and got a tour of the campus. Valerie was shown to her quarters, a small corner room in the staff dorm with views of the entire campus. She could see across to

Old Main and the wards, down to the carriage house and the piggery behind the garages. It was a strange sort of beautiful with its brick towers and fenced-in porches. Ignoring its function you could almost see the hospital as an extension of Smith College, the buildings dressed in the same Elizabethan red and surrounded by lush green lawns landscaped to perfection.

Valerie dropped her bags on the floor and started unpacking, filling the tiny bureau, then hanging her dresses and her new uniform in the closet. The narrow metal bed was spread up but Valerie could see she would need another blanket to ward off the chill that seeped through the walls. She glanced at her watch just as the lunch bell rang and picked her way across campus to the cafeteria, a soaring, airy space with cathedral ceilings and oval-shaped windows overlooking the male nurses' quarters. As she stood in the doorway surveying the tables, much like the first day of school, scouting where she should sit, a blow to the shoulder sent her pitching forward into space. Valerie braced herself for an explosion of pain but she never hit the floor. A strong hand wrapped around her waist and pulled her back, setting her flat on her feet.

A man in a white coat held her steady and though she didn't intend to stare, she found herself taking in his neat brown hair, cleanly trimmed mustache, and straight white teeth set into a wide, laughing smile. "My apologies miss, I didn't see you behind me."

"Quite alright sir. I'm fine, though a bit embarrassed by my lack of composure."

He let out a short, round laugh. "No it was absolutely my fault. You must be new."

"I am. Valerie Martin." She dipped her chin and smiled briefly.

"Pleasure to meet you Miss Martin. I'm Robert Willard, one of the docs here."

"Pleasure to meet you as well Dr. Willard."

"Please, call me Robert," he said, smiling rather too intently. "Enjoy your lunch."

She watched as Dr. Willard-- rather Robert- made the circuit of the room, greeting staff and patients alike. Valerie sidled up to the buffet where she grabbed a tray and perused the meal options, some of which looked quite good.

"Stay away from anything called 'chowder' or 'casserole'." A young woman who looked to be about Valerie's age, wearing a sardonic smirk and a ratty gray cardigan over her uniform reached over Valerie and pointed out the offending dishes. "I'm Marian, your next door neighbor in the staff ward." Marian didn't have the poise or diction of a college girl. Her black hair was rolled back in a very stylish puff and she wore dark lipstick with a touch of red rouge on her high cheekbones and she had startling blue eyes the color of winter sky. "Grab a plate and I'll fill you in on all the gory details."

Valerie nodded dumbly, struck by the sheer volume of words that poured forth from this girl's mouth, but she also found herself smiling at this brazen little thing standing next to her. She followed Marian to a table and sat, spreading a napkin over her lap and taking a bite of the quiche she had chosen and immediately began to choke.

Marian laughed, a raucous barking laugh, and pointed to Valerie's plate. "Makes you wonder if it isn't the food that makes them crazy."

Laughing, Valerie dropped her fork and took a sip of milk. "That really is foul."

"Indeed it is!" Marian grabbed Valerie's plate and pushed it to the end of the table where it was quickly taken away by a patient. Noting Valerie's look of surprise, Marian explained quickly. "They all have posts. The healthier ones work all over the hospital, most of them in the kitchen and gardens."

"Interesting. I never would have thought they could be trusted like that."

Marian shrugged. "Some of them can."

Valerie looked around at the staff and patients buzzing around the cafeteria and caught sight of Dr. Willard on the opposite side of the room talking to a young female staffer. Valerie felt her face warm as she watched him move closer and touch her arm as he spoke.

"Ah, so you've spotted the fox in our henhouse then." Marian stood, waiting for Valerie to finish her milk. "He's married. To a foreign girl."

"Oh, no. I was just..."

"I know you were just. And I was just too. Come on." Marian led Valerie through the sea of white coats and hospital garb. She headed for an arched opening in the brick wall labeled "Tunnel" with an arrow pointing straight ahead.

"Where are we going?" Valerie asked.

"Back to the staff ward. The easy way." Together they descended a flight of stairs into the dark, then emerged in a tight, red brick hallway with windows above their heads. "Right now we're under the first floor patient wards."

Amazing. Just the idea that they were now under the hospital, that there were people moving around right over their heads fascinated Val. In a few places there were doors set into the walls with labels like "Records" or "Lab", but then Valerie noticed a door marked "Morgue".

"Is there really a morgue?"

Marian nodded. "Of course. That's where they handle the dead. It's haunted you know. Boo!" She turned and threw her hands up in Valerie's face, delighting in the look of horror on her new friend's face. "I'm kidding. But it is spooky at night. I try not to come down here after dark if I can help it."

They reached another stone arch marked "Staff Ward" with a narrow, twisting staircase that led to the dorm. Valerie followed Marian into her room where she gestured for Valerie to take a seat in the lone battered wooden chair. She sat and watched Marian flit around the room halfheartedly picking up discarded clothing and shoes; it looked as if she simply walked out of her clothing and left it where it fell. Valerie's mother would have had heart failure had her own daughter done the same, but it looked like Marian had not had a similar upbringing.

Marian reached into her sweater and pulled out a pack of cigarettes, tapped one out, and fished a lighter out a nearby desk drawer. Settling onto the edge of the unmade bed, Marian took a drag, then turned her gaze to Valerie. "So Val, are you ready for Hospital Hell?"

CHAPTER 3

Well into her first week back at Northampton Valerie had developed a sort of rhythm, a routine to the job. She created data sheets for the project and filed them neatly in a folder with a pad of paper on the side to take notes on if necessary. She pulled files five at a time but there were so many to get through that she wondered if she would make it through them all in good time, especially when she fell upon a name she recognized. Occasionally she would pause at one she knew and try to picture the ward in her head.

The first was Patricia Ackerman who had been diagnosed with hysteria and had been in the first room on the right on B Ward. Patricia was considered one of the "easier" patients as she was relatively quiet and always eager to help out on the ward. The only thing that had grated on Valerie's nerves was Patricia's incessant weeping and calling out for her husband; coincidentally it was he who had her committed so he could take up with a mistress ten years his junior. Valerie marked down the information needed and returned Patricia's file to the stack.

Another, Elizabeth Andrews, was in her sixties and was confined to Northampton State Hospital for most of her life after setting fire to her parents' bedroom as they slept. While in hospital she developed a penchant for stealing things and made off with whatever she could get her hands on- silverware, bits of paper, books from the library. Once she even managed to pilfer a patient's sock off her foot as she ate her supper. Valerie wondered what had become of Elizabeth—Betsy as she liked to be called. She had been one of the first patients to leave NSH in the 1980's, bound for a specialized nursing home.

It was certainly slow going but it was also fostering in Valerie something resembling nostalgia as the names floated by, bringing twenty years of memories with them. It was late Friday when the name she had secretly dreaded surfaced amongst the C's-- Esme Carraway. By 1960 Val, as Marian insisted on calling her, had learned the ropes and was getting to know the ward. In December of that year Esme turned twelve; the second of her birthdays marked at the asylum. Her mother had committed her at the age of ten; back then it was common practice to institutionalize children with adults. Two years before, her father had passed away and Esme fell into a depression, eating little, speaking to no one. Mrs. Carraway tried everything she could to bring Esme back into the world but the child stubbornly refused to surface from her misery.

Shortly after committing her daughter, Mrs. Carraway passed away as well and there was no other family to claim the child. Esme's care was transferred to the state, leaving her alone and forgotten. Valerie was the only staffer Esme seemed to warm to, touching Valerie's hand when she tucked the child in, leaving Valerie little gifts-- pieces of sketches or sculptures made from the detritus lying around the ward. But of course no one visited, no mail ever came for her like it did for others, and it broke Valerie's heart to watch the child at mail call, waiting eagerly, only to have her hopes dashed. Valerie began walking into town and buying postcards with different animals on them, posting them to Esme from the mailbox on Main Street. Other staffers scoffed, calling it a waste of four cents but Val couldn't care less. Though she never signed the cards, Esme would always turn and look at her with an impish smile before retreating to her room with her newest treasure, thanking Valerie with a sketch, a few of which she was certain she still had packed away somewhere. They were now all that was left of the child.

Esme's eventual death had nearly broken Valerie's heart; sometimes she could still feel that crushing blow to the chest, the one she had felt the night Marian had woken her from a dead sleep, tears streaming down her face, telling her that Esme had killed herself. They said she was found hanging from her bed sheets, looped over and around the heavy metal light fixture in her room. Even now, standing in the basement of the Haskell Building clutching Esme's notarized death certificate in her hand Valerie still had a difficult time accepting that Esme had chosen to end her life, but then one never knew what lurked in the hearts of the mentally ill.

Having recorded the necessary data, Valerie wiped away the moisture in her eyes and put the files back in the cabinet, pulling out another stack of five. Her memories of many of the other patients were foggy at best but scanning their records brought back snippets here and there. Susan Bradford-- Valerie remembered her as a hell raiser who showed up on the ward in 1968. She was the wild, willful daughter of wealthy conservative social climbers who had no idea how to control their child and so had her committed. She hadn't belonged in an institution, not by modern standards, but back then it was far easier to commit a burdensome family member and patients like Susan were treated with outrageous levels of antipsychotic medications or worse, electroshock therapy. Those were the dark days, days when the staff often imagined themselves to be just as crazy as the patients.

Valerie glanced at the clock, realizing that it was nearing 5:00 and Bill hadn't come to check on her once, not that she had expected as much. Opening one last file folder, Valerie ran her thumb over the patient's photo-- a young girl named Ashley Collins who looked a great deal like Esme. Valerie vaguely remembered Ashley who had only had a brief stay on the ward in the early 1970's, but she couldn't for the life of her remember what had become of Ashley. Flipping to the back of the file she scanned the pages until she came to the discharge section. Condition Upon Discharge: Death due to manual asphyxiation. Hanging.

Like Esme, Ashley was reported as being found hanging from her bed sheets, her neck broken. Turning to the blue intake notes in the front, Valerie read through the lines of handwritten notes, searching for the name of Ashley's assigned doctor and lo and behold—

"Dr. Willard." Valerie had spoken his name aloud, her trembling fingers on her lips. Both overseen by Robert Willard, a coincidence that set Valerie's teeth on edge.

Valerie wasn't certain what that meant but something made her head begin to rattle around, searching for a place to click. She pulled out a clean sheet of typing paper where she wrote Ashley Collins' name alongside Dr. Willard's with a question mark. She returned the files to the drawer and tucked the piece of paper with Ashley's name into an empty folder, stashing it in her purse. She locked each cabinet, gathered her things, and pulled the door shut behind her, leaving the ghost of Dr. Willard locked inside with the girls.

CHAPTER 4

Outside the temperature had dropped substantially and the air smelled of an early snow. She found that as she walked she could not stop thinking about both Esme and Ashley Collins, wondering at what appeared to be a tenuous connection at best. The two girls had a similar physical appearance and according to their files, had curable diagnoses and were being treated with an eye to eventual release. It was the similarities in the manner of their deaths that bothered Valerie most. The longer Valerie had spent on the wards the more she had become fascinated with the ways in which each woman's illness eventually broke her down. Though many of them were diagnosed similarly, each manifested their symptoms differently and each faced their futures-- or lack thereof-- in unique ways. Every once in awhile Valerie imagined she caught a glimpse of who they had been before their illness had ruined them, but it was only a rare moment of clarity before they retreated into their hysterias and delusions; it made her inconsolably sad.

In the late 1960's there were at least two intakes for every one discharge and the wards grew to be a sort of living hell, a snake pit where nothing was truly accomplished beyond maintaining the most basic level of safety and even that was tenuous at best. Most times Valerie looked back on her transfer to Westborough as more of a relief than a sadness, a pardon from watching the Northampton she loved crumble around her. It seemed that her life at the asylum had existed in a sort of parallel reality; the memories had grown cloudy and soft around the edges but her memories of the filth and sadness were clear as day. Still, it didn't explain the sudden suicides of two young girls who, for all intents and purposes had the rest of their lives before them.

31

Letting herself into the cottage she shrugged off her coat and changed out of her dress. She threw on flannel pajamas and padded back to the kitchen in her slippers to put on the teakettle. As she waited for it to boil she brooded. She wondered why the suicides were ringing every one of her internal alarm bells but the more she turned it over in her head, the more she felt that something wasn't quite right.

Dr. Willard wasn't quite right, he never had been. Her initial impressions of the doctor had left her wary of him; he had unnerved her, but not in the way he had the other women at the hospital, who wore their hearts on their sleeves and openly worshiped him. Valerie instead admitted that she had not found him the least bit attractive beyond his physical appearance. She had suspected—and rightly so it turned out- that he was not an honest man. When she was still new to the ward, Valerie had not been privy to the idle gossip of the other girls, but one afternoon, a few years into her tenure on Ward B, she, Marian, Allison, and Lily Wallace walked through the declining daylight to the cafeteria before second shift and Allison began to let her lips run wild.

"Did you hear Lorraine Moody quit?"

Marian smirked. "I'm not surprised."

"Why not?" Val asked, tucking her hands into her sweater pockets.

"Well because she just got left cold," Lily Wallace added.

Val shook her head and sighed. "That is why you should never take up with fellow staff members."

"It wasn't just any staffer Val," Marian laughed. "It was Dr. Willard."

Valerie felt herself recoil with disgust. "But he's married."

"So he is," Marian said, still chuckling. She linked her arm with Val's as they walked and looked up at the star choked sky. "He'll move on to someone new in short order. Mark my words."

All of her suspicions about Dr. Willard were confirmed by Marian's casual assessment of the situation that evening, and part of Val wanted very badly to confront Dr. Willard and scold him for thinking he could use his title and his white coat to lure women who weren't his wife. As Marian predicted, Lorraine Moody was not Robert's last transgression and certainly had not been his first; Val wanted no part of his game playing and from that evening on, she studiously ignored and avoided the good doctor. Unfortunately for her he seemed to have a sixth sense for, and strong attraction to women who would be hard won. Valerie found him to be conspicuously present wherever she was and one day he approached her in the cafeteria as she ate with the girls.

"Excuse me Miss Martin. May I speak with you?"

Val glanced around the table searching for an excuse to tell him no but none came to her.

"Yes sir." She stood from the table and lamely followed Dr. Willard out of the cafeteria and into an alcove in the hallway where he turned abruptly to face her.

"Miss Marin I get the distinct impression that you're avoiding me."

Valerie looked him straight in the eye. "Yes sir. I am."

"Why? And why are you calling me sir? I told you to call me Robert."
        "That, sir, would be unprofessional. Though it seems your lines of propriety are rather blurred."

"What on earth are you talking about?"

By God, he actually had the nerve to look incredulous! Val narrowed her eyes and felt the red blush of anger creep to her cheeks. "The girls talk, sir."

"The girls talk eh?" He said with an attempt at lightening the mood of the conversation. "And what are they talking about these days?"

"You. And Lorraine Moody."

"Ah, I see," he said with a sigh. "I should have guessed as much." He crossed his arms over his chest and leaned against the wall. "It's not true Valerie."

"I doubt that very much Dr. Willard and I would prefer it if you called me Miss Martin."

Dr. Willard's mouth sagged open. "It is not true! Yes, Lorraine Moody did have a crush on me that much is so, but I rebuffed her. She tried to slander me by saying we were having an affair, but we absolutely were not."

Val shook her head and laughed scornfully. "It does not make you a better man to lay blame at the feet of the woman. And I'm told this is not the first time you've strayed."

He looked defeated for a moment. "That is true. I did once have a relationship with a woman here but you have to understand, my wife and I do not have a traditional marriage.

Putting up a hand to stem the tide of excuses, Val shook her head. "Dr. Willard, you seem to have mistaken me for a woman who wants to hear your explanations."

"Julia is a German Jew. She left her country as a child during the war to live with our neighbors, distant relations of some sort. I got to know her quite well. As the war ended Julia was frightened that she would be deported or sent to a camp here in the United States like they did with the Japanese. She said the only way she would be safe would be to marry an American man." He shrugged as if to say, and there I was.

"So you married a woman you didn't love. It's still a marriage vow, not to be taken lightly."

"Oh I love Julia. Just not as a wife, more as a sister. So I agreed to marry her and take care of her."

"You're not making your case much better Dr. Willard." Valerie turned on her heel and walked away, leaving him dumbstruck.

The force of the memory surprised her. She recalled how she had trembled as she gave Dr. Willard that tongue-lashing and though it was a first for her; she was generally rather even-tempered, but something about Dr. Willard stoked a bitter flame of anger within her and it wouldn't be the last time she would go toe to toe with that man. She washed out her teacup and set it out to dry on the mat, then climbed into bed willing her mind to calm itself, but instead she lay awake until the small hours of the morning. It was nearing 1:00 am when her eyelids finally fell in on themselves and she slept well into daylight.

When she rose that Saturday morning, Valerie felt an almost physical pull from the hospital buildings. She dressed in jeans and a warm sweater, then layered on her coat, scarf, and hat. Locking the cottage behind her, she slipped on her gloves and headed in the direction of the hill where she found the front gate gone; only the brick pillars remained. To the right the doctors' houses sat so choked with weeds that they were barely visible, even now on the edge of winter. Behind the fences, vines and brittle brown branches clung to the buildings, reaching up their walls all the way to their roof lines.

Walking slowly up the drive Val frowned at the eerie panorama-- it was like looking at an old stereoscopic image superimposed over the decaying landscape; the "then" in her head laid over the "now" in front of her. She stood under the cafeteria walkway, scuffing the toe of her boot against the weeds that sprouted out of the cracks in the asphalt, looking up at the cracked and broken glass, the sun ravaging the red of the brick. She followed the fence to the right, around to the front of Old Main, past the green potter's shed with its door wide open, hanging listlessly to one side. It made her cold to see the grand portico gone; it had long since collapsed the bits and pieces carted away to a salvage yard. Where the front entrance once was there were now maroon-painted plywood boards riveted in place, pasted with "No Trespassing" signs.

She turned to look for the wrought iron fountain and caught a glimpse of it hidden in the brambles, swatches of black peeking through here and there, and she thought what a shame it was that they hadn't done something to protect it from the elements. A breeze kicked up, bending the tall grasses and reminding Valerie of a child's hiding place, a secret garden of sorts. She walked closer to the fence and laced her fingers through the chain links, gazing up at the windows and trying to remember what offices had been where. As she looked in the direction of the wards she was surprised to see a hole in the fence where it looked as if the links had been cut and pulled aside so that someone could slip through. Valerie followed the fence line until she reached the cut and ducked through the fence, heading up a well-worn path to a door that was just open enough to slide her fingers behind. With a mighty pull the door popped open and Val found herself inside the hospital for the first time in over fifteen years. She stopped just inside the doorway for a moment to listen; first and foremost to make sure she was alone, but also because a part of her expected to hear the sounds of the hospital still in motion.

The door Valerie had entered through was a fire door leading to two sets of stairs-- one to the basement and the tunnels below, and one set of three concrete stairs ascending to the main floor. Valerie headed up then left towards the lobby, curious to see what had become of the grand foyer but she was stopped by a cavernous hole that stretched, open-mouthed across

Old Main's entire expanse, through which she could see straight down to the basement. All three ceilings above had collapsed, creating a massive crater in the floor with debris of all sorts sticking out.

She had only ever entered through Old Main once since the day of her interview; she and the other girls in her dorm always entered through the cafeteria or tunnels, yet she remembered the lobby as if it was yesterday. Turning away from the wreckage, Valerie headed down the murky hallway to the stairs and climbed to the second floor where B Ward was nearly unrecognizable. The nurses' station had been renovated at some point to accommodate computers and the shelves of handwritten ward books had been replaced by binders of printouts, the thick, threaded glass had been removed and the windows were now sheets of high impact plexi that would never shatter, not until the wrecking ball came through.

Valerie headed down the hall, past the day room, and down the patient hallway, moving slowly, touching each of the doors she passed until she came to Esme's room; the door was new and smooth, no longer the heavy old wooden door with the diamond-shaped window and thick white wash. She could have continued on her way but instead she stepped into Esme's room and looked around, the powder blue paint peeling off in sheets. The walls had been there. The walls had known Esme, she had lived within them, then died within them. Valerie reached out to touch the nearest one and a paint chip snapped off. She ran her hands across the crumbling plaster, watching the sky blue skin slough off and float through the air, settling in a pile at her feet. Slipping a chunk of paint into her pocket, Valerie turned to leave, closing the door as if she had just finished room checks.

There was nothing left for her to see of the hospital and it broke her heart to see it in such decay. Outside the sun was high in the sky, the air carrying the snap of approaching winter. Valerie ducked back under the fence and headed left this time, passing the tip of the ward wing and heading toward the staff dorm that was boarded up tight with a metal bar across the door, which was just fine with her. She'd seen quite enough.

CHAPTER 5

The first snow in Northampton was always a beautiful affair. The town had become a glittering white blanket of winter glow, the buildings coated in cottony drifts. Valerie enjoyed walking to work that Monday, stopping to listen to the snow falling through the frozen silence. She passed Bill on her way down to the file room but he barely looked at her, giving her a tight smile that she briefly returned. It seemed the novelty of her presence had worn off and they had returned to the strained silence that had marked their working relationship for years.

Bill Dunston had joined Valerie on the wards at Northampton in 1961. It was early spring and change was in the air and not just amongst the staff. The administration was shifting too; Mrs. Harding in hiring had been replaced by a tiny, bespectacled man named Mr. Goldstern who offered Valerie a raise and apologized for the hospital's oversight of its female staffers-- it was an increase to $3.00 an hour with time and a half on Sundays. She remembered feeling as if that raise had won her something of a small victory over the bureaucracy that controlled Northampton State, though when she looked back, she realized the elation was short lived. In a matter of years, the bureaucracy would come out on top—not Valerie.

That was also the day that Bill arrived on B Ward. Val was finishing up room checks, greeting each woman in turn, then heading for the day room just as the visitor's bell sounded. The head nurse, Mrs.Korsinsky rose from her chair in the nurses' station and went to the double doors at the end of the hall, pulling her massive key ring from her pocket to unlock the doors. Waiting on the other side were two clean cut, nervous looking young men and Mrs. Korsinsky led them into the wards, locking the door behind them. One of the young men glanced fearfully over his shoulder as the head nurse's key clanged loudly in the lock and Val swore she saw him flinch.

"Miss Martin, this is Mr. William Dunson and Mr. Lawrence Porter." Mrs. Korsinsky gestured to each man in turn, then led them both away to give them a tour of the ward.

Bill-- the flincher. He was tall, thin, and nervous, barely knowing where he began and ended. He bumped into things and frequently tripped over himself but once he settled in he eventually developed enough confidence to ask Val on a number of dates, all of which she declined. Funny, she didn't remember much about the other young man, Lawrence Porter, other than how handsome he was, though she never did see him again after that day.

Each time Bill asked Val on a date the stronger he reeked of desperation. He wanted to settle down and not because he was a romantic, but because he was dependent. He had no essence of his own and he seemed to be convinced that having a wife would complete him, give him the substance he lacked. Even then Val knew she wanted more from a man. She considered marriage a partnership, a union of strength; Bill viewed it as an acquisition. But Bill did not, would not understand her rejection. He firmly believed Valerie was simply handing out excuses, hiding behind her love for another man and in his tortured imagination that man was Robert Willard.

Before the year was out Bill was reassigned to the surgical ward. He showed amazing skill in the midst of a medical emergency when Betsy Flint, a seizure patient whose illness had done a great deal of damage to her brain, had a seizure so violent that she managed to slice herself wide open on the sharp edge of a table and began bleeding profusely in the middle of the day room.

Bill had jumped in immediately, pulling off his tie and creating a makeshift tourniquet which he wrapped around the woman's neck to stop the bleeding that seemed to be coming from everywhere all at once. Somehow Bill had recognized that it was pouring from a gash in her throat and though it was imperative the bleeding be stopped immediately, the poor woman was still seizing, writhing on the floor and jack knifing from one position to the next while making the most grotesque faces anyone had ever seen on a human being. Bill had deftly turned her on her side to keep her from choking on her own tongue while also keeping her from bleeding to death.

When the doctors came rushing in from surgical, Bill refused to take his hands off of Betsy's still bleeding throat and so they put her on a gurney and Bill climbed on top of her, his hands still clasped as blood bubbled through his fingers, and rode the gurney all the way to surgical. The story goes that he remained in that position until the doctors had her hooked to an IV and began to clean her wounds, lifting his hands a little at a time so that they could work carefully around his fingers. Bill saved Betsy Flint's life.

Valerie now stood in the basement of the Haskell Building, the radiators singing with the effort of throttling steam to all three floors of the building, making the file room a steamy nest of sorts. She shed her coat and got down to work, her spreadsheets looking mighty grim, page after page of hash marks, and double, sometimes triple digit numbers filling the tiny boxes. She wondered if she and Bill would ever be able to be in the same room together without wanting to claw each other's eyes out, but it seemed he planned to ignore her. No, she would not be able to confide in him; she had continued to keep her own private tally on a separate piece of paper, ticking off her suspicions from the previous week. As of that morning Valerie had marked down six girls who had died during Robert Willard's tenure, all six previously noted as progressing toward eventual discharge; all six done in by their own hand. It was clearly not quite what she had expected to find when assigned this particular task but there it was in black and white. And further, it couldn't possibly be coincidence that each one had been attended by Dr. Willard.

At lunch Valerie closed and locked the door so she could return to the girls' files without fear of being disturbed. She wasn't entirely sure what it was she was searching for but she wondered if rereading each file might lead her to some sort of reasonable explanation. Leaving Esme's file for last, Valerie reopened Ashley Collins. According to her intake form Ashley was admitted to hospital in 1970 following a nervous breakdown at a cocktail party her parents had hosted in celebration of her acceptance to Mount Holyoke College; she would be the first woman in her family to attend higher education. Halfway through the party her parents noted Ashley's conspicuous absence and were devastated to find their only child collapsed on the bathroom floor in her party dress, a half empty bottle of sleeping pills beside her. The guests were dispatched with appropriately vague apologies and Ashley was delivered to Northampton that evening.

Stopping to take a bite of the sandwich she had fetched from the cafeteria, Valerie skipped ahead to the treatment notes in the middle of the file. By all accounts Ashely had recovered well from her breakdown, stabilizing quickly with only a modicum of medication and regular meetings with Dr. Willard, none of which Valerie found curious. What did raise a red flag was a note from Nurse Ryland, the charge nurse, written in her tiny, cramped hand at the bottom of one of the ward reports, noting that Dr. Willard would often stop to visit Ashley rather late at night.

Though Valerie certainly could not divine the woman's intentions from her pencil strokes, she had known Curran Ryland well enough to know that if she had taken time away from her charges to write this bit down, that meant she found it out of turn for Dr. Willard to be visiting. It was noted however that Ashley continued to progress and Dr. Willard's final note suggested that the girl might be ready to go home in time for her first semester at Mount Holyoke, yet soon after she would be found hanging from her light fixture, just like Esme.

The next file Valerie set before her was that of Margaret Tanner. Margaret appeared to be a far more complicated case, diagnosed as a paranoid schizophrenic and committed to Northampton in the mid-1960's after she suffocated her two young children in their beds. Her husband had come home one evening to find her at the kitchen table reading a book, cool as anything, and when he asked her where the children were she gestured vaguely in the direction of their room, picked up the lit cigarette that sat smoldering in the ashtray before her, and put it to her lips. Mr. Tanner would say later in an interview with the doctors that he had never before seen his wife smoke; the fact that she was doing so that day had struck him so at that moment that he just knew something terrible had happened. And so it had, he found, when he looked in on his children who were both now quite dead indeed.

Margaret had been admitted to C Ward, the violent ward, which was why Valerie was unfamiliar with the woman's case. Mrs. Tanner was kept in solitary confinement for the better part of each day, allowed out only to bathe herself, and even then she was to be observed closely by a staff member at all times. Her room, if Valerie remembered correctly, most likely would have been stripped of all human comforts with bed bolted to the floor, window barred and shrouded by metal screening, the light fixture secured to the ceiling and surrounded by a metal cage. The rooms in C Ward, the violent ward, had no closets, no extraneous furniture. Margaret would not have even been allowed a book for fear she could do damage to herself or others with its various parts.

Most of the physicians at Northampton saw patients on one ward, and one ward only. Dr. Robert Willard was one of the few exceptions to that rule; he carried a caseload of both male and female patients on a number of wards, and so he was assigned to Margaret Tanner's case. His notes were meticulous and many, as the woman's case seemed to be quite a trial for him. She was a complicated woman who also seemed to have no memory of what she'd done.

In their sessions Mrs. Tanner would regale Dr. Willard with tales of dinner parties, films she had seen with her husband, and recitals at her children's school. She spoke of every minute that led up to the murder of her children but it was there her conscious mind seemed to separate from reality, and she would simply skip over that entire evening. In fact, Margaret Tanner, over the entire length of her stay at the hospital, seemed to not even be aware of where she was. She seemed utterly convinced she was at a day spa, there to take respite from her busy life as a wife and mother.

In all likelihood her suicide was not entirely a surprise. Schizophrenics often committed suicide purely by accident, not realizing the permanence of the act, and Mrs. Tanner was likely no exception. The night she died she had somehow managed to procure an item that was almost unheard of on C Ward: a razor blade. She probably never meant to cut deep enough to end her life, just deep enough to ease a bit of her pain but her regular bathroom attendant who was vigilant in thwarting her patient's regular attempts was out sick and the woman filling in, slightly less vigilant, had fallen asleep while Margaret bathed. The nurse woke to find the poor woman lying in a tub of tepid crimson water.

Strangely enough, when Valerie looked closely at the ward nurse's reports in Margaret's file, a woman Valerie had never met, she too had noted the frequency of Dr. Willard's nightly visits. As much as she would have liked to have been just the slightest bit surprised, Valerie found that she was not. She had learned, at the hand of Dr. Willard himself that people often weren't what they seemed and so, as she considered the implications of her discovery, found that she felt only disgust.

That evening Valerie bundled up her work, closed and locked the filing cabinets, and gathered her belongings. She was still troubled by her suspicions and was so wrapped up in her thoughts that she didn't notice Bill standing in the doorway watching her put on her coat.

"How is it going?" He asked, startling her quite badly.

Val cleared her throat and buttoned her jacket. "It's going fine. Slow and tedious, as expected."

Bill nodded and crossed his arms over his chest, leaning against the door jamb. "I meant to check on you earlier but…" He trailed off as if Valerie should know the reason he hadn't checked on her. The tension between them was certainly reason enough for them to continue to avoid one another.

"Bill I..." Val took a step forward intending to gently broach the subject of the girls' deaths, but Bill instinctively stepped back.

"Valerie, I don't want to hear it," he said, shaking his head while staring at his shoes. "I only called you about this position because you were the only one left I could trust to do this job."

Valerie instantly felt her anger rise. As a rule, she tried not to let her emotions get the better of her but once in a great while attitudes like Bill's sparked her fury. "Bill! Enough! I have had enough of your lousy behavior!" she spat, stomping her foot on the carpeted floor for emphasis. The subject of the girls forgotten, Valerie let loose on Bill. "When will you understand that nothing, nothing I told you back then was an excuse? You have absolutely no idea what you are talking about and yet you insist on treating me with so little respect. Can you not grasp that perhaps, thirty years ago mind you, that I just did not feel the same way about you? That I simply wasn't interested?"

"Now you know..."

"No. No! I'm tired of you telling me what I know Bill. I tried to make you understand that I was only twenty years old, eight years your junior, and that I did not have feelings for you. Your ego just couldn't handle that, could it? You just couldn't imagine that I might turn down such an offer as marriage to the great William Dunston so you insisted on insulting me instead. Well, have I got news for you. I have always had my own mind and made my own decisions, independent of a man." By the time Val had stopped ranting Bill was looking rather shell shocked.

"Frances left me."

"What?" Valerie marveled at his abrupt shift in topic but recovered her senses quickly.
"Your wife left you? Why?"

"She said it was about time I learned how to be on my own." He hung his head and shifted his arms so he could dig his hands into the pockets of his brown corduroys.

Val let out an involuntary snort of laughter. "I can't say that I'm surprised."

Bill looked up, his mouth hanging open. "What is that supposed to mean?"

"Bill, listen," Val said, putting her things back down and pulling out two chairs. She motioned for him to sit and watched as he slouched into a seat. "Part of the reason I was never attracted to you was because it was obvious you needed someone who was willing to do for you and no one else."

"Well of course I wouldn't want any wife of mine doing for someone else!"

Val sighed in frustration. "I don't mean doing for another man. I mean doing for herself as well. You wanted someone who would forsake her own personality in order to serve yours. It was plain as day! And though it might have taken her a bit longer to discover, Frances obviously grew to feel the same way."

"You're calling me selfish, aren't you?"

"Well yes, if the shoe fits," Val agreed, sitting back in her chair and crossing one leg neatly over the other. Val looked carefully at Bill, her eyes narrowed. "You spent thirty years resenting me because you thought I rejected you for another man instead of opening your ears and listening to what I had to say. My feeling is that you may have done a bit of the same in your marriage."

Burying his face in his hands, Bill groaned with what Val could only interpret as a level of sorrow, perhaps mixed with a measure of shame. "I've treated her terribly. God, I treated you terribly."

"Yes Bill, you have," Valerie laughed and a tiny chuckle escaped through Bill's fingers.

"I must have insulted you terribly by accusing you of having an affair with Robert Willard. It was just that I had heard so many rumors of him with other women that when I saw you two together it was the logical conclusion. I suppose you're right though. My ego couldn't quite accept that you just didn't have feelings for me. There had to be another explanation and I firmly believed he was the reason you wouldn't agree to see me."

"Oh Bill, Robert Willard was a womanizer, but some women were smart enough to avoid his advances. I never would have involved myself with someone like him. I wanted a home and a family, not a cheap dalliance with a married coworker."

Bill sighed deeply and rubbed his eyes with the backs of his knuckles. "Oh how I hated that man. Do you remember the day I passed the two of you in the solarium? You were talking, your heads bent towards one another and I stopped. You looked up and saw me watching, then pushed him away as if I had caught you doing something untoward. It was then I decided you must have given in to him. To his charms."

She hadn't thought about that day in almost thirty years but it seemed Bill had thought about it often enough for both of them. Now here he was, pouring his heart out to her in the basement of the building that had come to define both their lives because, as it turned out, Bill had been sleeping on the couch in his office. Frances had asked him to leave and Bill had nowhere else to go. He had no friends other than those couples with whom he and Frances socialized together; he had never formed any sort of bond with any of the husbands, leaving all the arranging and planning to Frances. His brothers had moved away, calling only on holidays and even then they called only to speak to Frances. Bill had effectively isolated himself from everyone he had ever come in contact with.

That night, as Valerie walked home leaving Bill to trudge back to his office for another sleepless night, she wondered what it would be like to be so dependent on others to make you who you were, only to find one day that you had failed everyone, including yourself. Valerie had chosen to be alone but what was it like to have aloneness thrust upon you without your say so? She had a hard time putting herself in Bill's shoes and though she felt sorry for him in her own way, she couldn't bring herself to truly pity him for he had brought it on himself. He was, without doubt, selfish and pigheaded, qualities that made it quite difficult for Valerie to identify with him.

She was pleased however that she and Bill may have at least found some common ground in their working relationship, had reached some sort of détente. Bill seemed to have finally heard her side of things once and for all though she still felt as if he was hardly owed much consideration after the way he had behaved towards her for the better part of three decades. At the same time though she recognized that having cleared the air might make it easier to share the same work space.

The next morning Valerie woke to the second snow of the season, making it impossible to do much more than stay inside and tidy up, doing laundry in the basement of her apartment building. Pulling the last load out of the dryer, Valerie went back upstairs to put it all away. As she hung her sweaters in her closet, she noticed a box she had avoided unpacking since moving from Westborough, a rather large box she had pushed to the back of her closet and left there without even breaking the tape seal. It was a box full of memories, nearly thirty years' worth, including a photo album she had put together in the summer of 1961.

Val's birthday was the first of June and Marian had planned a bang up surprise party in her room, giving her a camera and two rolls of film. She said she bought it because she could see Val taking mental pictures of everything around her and she wanted her friend to be able to take lasting, permanent pictures.

"Someday you won't have such a flawless memory," Marian joked when Val was finished unwrapping it. "This way, you will never forget all those moments you might want to remember."

She bent to retrieve the box from her closet and took a pair of scissors to the tape. The photo album was right on top, an old burgundy leather bound book with black paper pages. After paying a fortune to develop the photographs she had spent hours painstakingly labeling each photo and pasting it inside with the sticky photo corners that you had to lick like an envelope to get them to adhere to the paper. The edges of the pages had begun to flake away and as Val lifted the album out of the box a few of the black and white images fluttered out of the book and onto the floor, their black corners stuck to the photos rather than to the book.

Sinking to her knees, Val gathered up the loose photos, running her fingertips over the smiling faces trapped in the tiny 2" by 2" square. Her knees quickly began to ache but rather than stand up and take the album to the living room couch like a grown woman should, Val slid to the floor with her back against the closet door, her knees drawn up so that she could flip through the album as she would have done thirty years ago with Marian beside her.

The first pages of photos had been taken on her birthday. Marian and Allison had arranged a surprise party in Lily Wallace's room, the last place Val would have expected. The surprise was a success and Val had been delighted to see how much effort her friends had put into the celebration. Marian had given her the camera that morning, along with two rolls of film, in anticipation of that evening's fete. Everyone was smiling and laughing, reaching out towards the camera as if reaching from the photograph itself to touch her. At some point in the evening Valerie must have handed the camera off to someone else because there were also plenty of pictures of her with her friends. Looking at those photos Val remembered how happy she had been that night.

Other pages were filled with photos of the women outside in the garden that summer. The weather had slowly drifted toward summer on a rolling wave of heat that brushed spring aside, turning the ward into a veritable convection oven. Val, along with a few of the junior ward girls tried to take the patients out as often as possible in the afternoons, taking strolls through the gardens, helping the farm staff with the animals and the crops. Esme would flit from stall to stall, patting the cows on the head and feeding the chickens. Another patient, Caroline, had developed something of a crush of one of the farms hands, a townie who came in every morning to tend the animals though he was easily fifteen years her junior. Val loved being out of doors with the women. The fresh air did them good, as did the change of scenery. She firmly believed that staring at the same four walls for hours on end was not good for the mind, and though it was certainly no cure for insanity, Val believed that being so close to nature was good for the soul.

She encouraged the women to dig their bare hands deep into the dirt and it was quite the sight to see, these broken human shells tucking their skirts under their knees and crowing with delight as they plunged their fingers into the cool soil, letting it settle under their fingernails and dry crusty on their skin. Their joy was compounded when they would come out to see tiny green signs of growth pushing up where before there had been nothing but dust. Creating life, even on this most basic level, lifted their spirits and allowed them to feel the glow of accomplishment.

In one or two of the photos, a few of the women smiled and looked directly at the camera, but most did not. They gazed off into the distance, thinking their own private thoughts, barely even registering Val's presence. Mixed in with the portraits were also a few more artistic photos of the wards, photos that now seemed quite eerie—empty chairs, empty beds, and empty rooms. So many years later those images were quite an accurate portrayal of how the wards felt at times, and certainly how they looked now that the hospital was abandoned.

Reaching the end of the album, Val closed it and leaned her head back, smiling. She marveled at how young they all were. No wrinkles, no gray hair, no extra pounds lurking around their waistlines. Rising to her knees Valerie stowed the album, tucking it carefully back in its box, pushing the whole thing back into the closet. That night she slept soundly, her dreams peppered with flashes of smiles and the sunlight of what few good memories remained.

Valerie did remember that day, quite clearly in fact. She remembered walking to the ward to find Dr. Willard propping the door open with his shoulder, watching her approach.

"Good morning Miss Martin. I need to speak with you please."

Dr. Willard grabbed Valerie's elbow, steering her to the stairs and up to the second floor solarium. Pulling her inside, he turned to face her, looking as if he was angry enough to spit in her face.

"Why are you treating me this way?" he blurted, still holding onto her arm.

Valerie was so taken aback by his outburst that she couldn't speak.

"You must know by now that I have feelings for you."

Valerie didn't immediately realize how close Dr. Willard had gotten; his chin nearly brushing her forehead, his breath hot on her cheek as he harangued her, and that was when Bill had appeared in the doorway, staring at the two of them, his mouth open. His face went pale and Valerie knew beyond a doubt that he had misinterpreted what he had just seen. The doctor turned to see what it was she was looking at, allowing Valerie to take advantage of the break in the moment to push roughly past both him and Bill, escaping out into the hallway.

CHAPTER 6

On Monday Valerie rose, dressed, and headed back to the Haskell building. Try as she might she still had not found any more tenable connection between the girls, though she had puzzled over it all weekend. She tried her best to focus on the others, continuing to plow through the overflowing cabinets, but by lunch time Valerie's stomach was starting to grumble as she closed yet another drawer and filled a few more check boxes. She intended to go up to the cafeteria for lunch, but before she could Bill appeared at the door with his car keys in hand. He looked nervous, his lower lip tucked between his teeth, his fingers twisting in front of him. Valerie wondered if he had made any headway in getting Frances to take him back, hoping he might take a stab at becoming a bit more independent.

"What can I do for you Bill?"

"Well," he shifted from one foot to the other, put his hands in his pockets then took them out. "I was headed down to Fitzwilly's for lunch and wondered if you'd like to tag along. Talk about the job. Or something."

Valerie opened her mouth to decline but instead found herself accepting his invitation. "Sure," she said, pushing the girls' files under a stack of charts. "I think a long lunch is just what the doctor ordered."

Shrugging into her coat Valerie followed Bill out to the parking lot and climbed into his Volvo. Fitzwilly's was snugged up next to the railway overpass in a brick row building with green awnings. Inside Bill and Valerie were led to a small table in the window overlooking Main Street. It was a bit more intimate than Valerie would have liked but she was hungry and the food at Fitzwilly's was well worth it. Bill, however was visibly uncomfortable.

"I've always like this place," Bill said, clearing his throat and looking out the window at the cars crawling slowly by. "I remember when this place opened back in the 70's. I used to come here for beers with the other surgical staff."

Val looked around at the dark wood accented with heavy bronze details and fixtures, a second floor overlooking the bar. "The food is excellent."

Bill nodded just as the waiter approached to hand them menus. "That it is. I have yet to meet a menu item I don't like!" he said, laughing feebly at his own joke.

Asking the waiter for a glass of red wine, Valerie opened the menu and studied it carefully. It was difficult to choose a dish when she was that hungry; she considered ordering dishes she wouldn't normally touch. It was almost impossible to narrow it down to just one dish.

"So how goes the data collection nightmare?" Bill interrupted, peering at her over the edge of his menu, his glasses sliding down the bridge of his nose.

Having settled on a club sandwich and soup, Valerie closed her menu and pushed it to the edge of the table. "I've gotten quite a bit recorded. I made it through about 60% of my former charges and a smaller chunk of A Ward."

"So just females so far?"

Valerie shrugged. "It just seemed to make more sense to do the females first. I knew them."

Nodding, Bill closed his menu and the waiter shuffled over to take their order. "Well it sounds like you're making fairly quick work of the project. I know it's tedious but as you're well aware that's what the department is famous for."

"Typical bureaucracy," Valerie shrugged.

"It must be quite a trip down memory lane," Bill said as the waiter placed their drinks in front of them. He took a sip of his beer, wiping his mouth on his napkin, then spreading it absentmindedly in his lap. Frances had trained him well.

Val took a deep swallow of her wine, enjoying the thick warmth that spread down her throat and through her chest. "Yes it certainly has. Especially the women I worked closely with."

"Like that little girl. What was her name?"

"Esme." Valerie was surprised that Bill remembered. "Yes. She was such a lovely child."

Bill nodded and took a sip of his beer. "It sounds like your time on the wards was well spent. Not like surgical."

"What do you mean?" Valerie always imagined surgical to be one of the most interesting wards in the hospital. Ward staff had the chance to observe or assist in surgeries, coma treatments, electroshock. "I would have thought you'd never run out of interesting things to participate in on surgical."

"I thought the same thing at first, but it was hard to stand by and watch every time the doctors came up with a new treatment."

"Why?" Valerie swirled her wine and watched it coat the sides of her glass in spidery streaks of burgundy.

Sighing, Bill took another healthy swig of his beer and swallowed hard. "We were there at the height of everything, the heyday of mental health treatment. In the beginning it seemed so exciting, all these breakthroughs in medications and therapy. But then…then came the surgeries." Bill paused for a moment, seeming to collect his thoughts. "I would hear the doctors talking about how they chose which patients to try new surgeries on. It was like they weren't even talking about human beings."

Bill stopped talking as the waiter slid their lunches onto the table. "Are we all set here folks?" the young man asked.

Valerie nodded. "Yes, we are, thank you very much."

The waiter nodded in return, then hurried off to the back where Valerie assumed his own lunch was waiting. She turned to Bill and gestured for him to keep talking. "You were saying? About the surgeries?"

"Oh yes." Bill forked a bit of pasta into his mouth and chewed carefully. "The doctors were using the toughest patients, the ones who had essentially been abandoned, and they were experimenting on them. Obviously not in the way most people think of medical experiments, but still it was unsettling."

He sat for a moment, fork suspended in midair. "They were doing what they thought was best with what little they had, but watching procedures like ice pick lobotomies and electroshock therapy made me feel like I was observing a group of mad scientists. I remember the first time I watched a doctor give a patient ECT. The machine was such a piece of crap that when the assisting orderly flipped the switch the electrical current traveled through the patient then back to the machine, giving the orderly a hell of a shock too."

Valerie laughed though it certainly wasn't meant to be funny. "I suppose that would change your feelings about surgical. Our ward was a far cry from that kind of barbarism. We had the advantage of occasionally being able to heal those women with a bit of nurturing."

"I'm sorry your experience wasn't what you had hoped."

Bill shrugged and looked down at his almost empty plate; Valerie still had half her sandwich left. "It's alright. Water under the bridge."

Val bobbed her head in agreement. "So true. Water under the bridge."

Finishing off their meals and their drinks, Bill reached for the check and tucked a few bills into the folder, then gave it to the waiter before Valerie could raise a stink about sharing the cost of lunch.

Returning to the Haskell Building, Valerie gave Bill a tiny wave and thanked him for lunch, more than ready to dive back into the files. She sifted through name after name, filling more sheets with inane data and stuffing files back into overflowing drawers. Then, just as she was about to quit for the day, another handwritten note from Nurse Ryland surfaced, again documenting a late night ward visit from Dr. Willard. The note was dated some time in 1962 when Valerie had been on the wards for nearly three years. It was the fourth note she had found and if she was a gambling woman she would bet even money that there were more buried somewhere. She wished she could ask Curran about those curious observations but Valerie knew Nurse Ryland had passed a year ago from cancer.

Valerie sat and tapped her pen on the open file in front of her she began to wonder what had become of some of the other staff members. Marian had chosen not to transfer to another hospital; instead she had agreed to go home to help her parents on their farm in upstate New York. The day she said good-bye Val was gob smacked by the realization that though Marian had become her closest friend at NSH, she knew almost nothing about her; she never would have guessed that Marian was a country mouse. Allison Marquart had gone to the new psych ward at Springfield Hospital and Lilly Wallace had taken a position at Butler Hospital in Rhode Island. She hadn't bothered keeping track of any of the others.

Once in awhile Valerie toyed briefly with the idea of looking for Marian though it was doubtful she was still living on her parent's farm. It occurred to Valerie that she wouldn't know what to say if she did find her old friend. What would they talk about after fifteen years? Was Marian married? Did she have children? Would they have anything in common? The hospital had been their only bond. Valerie thought back to some of the nights on the ward that seemed to have no end in sight, nights when she could feel the tension the moment she walked on shift but her easy friendship with Marian was a constant bright spot. She never was able to form that kind of bond with another person again. There were times when she blamed the hospital for stripping her of herself, destroying the outgoing, carefree young girl she had once been. But her rational self would then remind her that it was her fault, she had allowed the asylum to become the only parameters within which she might be defined.

When she had first moved to Westborough she allowed one of her coworkers to set her up on a blind date with her single, middle-aged brother whose name she couldn't remember. Valerie met him in a loud, smoky bar and sat next to him drinking soda water while he plowed through tumblers of whiskey and talked about his golden retriever. When he finally turned to Valerie and asked her what her story was, all she could think to tell him about was work.

"Wow," he said, laughing rudely. "Well, you know what they say, all work and no play…"

"What is that supposed to mean?"

By now her date was slurring ever so slightly, resting his chin in his hand as his elbow slowly slid across the bar. "It means you're boring. Do you have any hobbies? Pets? Any interests other than your awful job?"

Valerie had gotten up then and left her date snoozing on the bar. Through her anger she realized he was right to a degree. What did she have outside of the hospital? She hadn't written in years. There was a time when she had loved to draw but even that had gone by the wayside. She couldn't lay her hand on her camera if her life depended on it, if it had even survived the move. Now she was cooped up in the basement of the only piece of her past still standing, wrestling with facts and figures when she should be filling out retirement papers and planning a trip somewhere. Although she had no idea where she would go since she had never even been out of Massachusetts. The only time she had ever travelled was when she had to attend a training at another hospital.

Her coworkers at Westborough had learned quickly that Valerie wasn't interested in small talk or Friday afternoon drinks at the local watering hole. Word of her disastrous date with what's-his-name spread quietly through the office; no one offered to set her up again. She politely declined invitations to birthday parties, anniversary dinners, and most work functions until she found herself working long after everyone else had gone home to husbands, wives, kids, and friends. Valerie didn't even have a pet.

Opening another file Valerie wondered what life would have been like if she hadn't cut herself out of it so cleanly. She couldn't pinpoint the exact moment it happened because it seemed she had drifted away from everyone else slowly, but broken ties so thoroughly. If she was honest, she would say a lot of it had to do with Robert Willard and the way he had pursued her relentlessly. After a while she began to fear that all men were inherently loose with their morals and she found herself distancing herself from them even though she was surrounded by plenty of men who might be described as decent. Valerie just found it difficult to accept that some men were honest in their intentions.

Robert's firm, prominent signature took up the entire bottom portion of the intake form she was staring at, the cross on the "t" a dramatic slash that invaded the "w" of Willard, the loops of the l's thin and tall, like he had been.

It was as if Valerie could read everything she needed to know about him from the way he signed his name, underscored by his ego. Of course she knew that was ridiculous. The only reason she was thinking that way was because she knew Robert well and had witnessed his blind ambition firsthand, watching him climb the ranks at the hospital at the expense of anyone who stood in his way. Was she bitter? Perhaps.

Closing up the last of the files for the day, Valerie closed and locked everything just as she had the day before, and the day before that. She pulled on the same winter coat she had been wearing for nearly six years, grabbed her purse that was so old that it was beginning to fray at the edges, and walked out the door. She walked across the street to her little cottage and let herself in, then spent her evening preparing to do it all over again the next day.

CHAPTER 7

Some nights on the wards were hell. By rights, second shift should have been quiet as the patients were meant to be asleep by 9:00, but in reality night was the worst time for those women; the darkness brought a fear that was absent in the light of day. At times that darkness compounded the depression or carried out the demons that only showed themselves after sundown. Some just quietly cried themselves to sleep. Others screamed and wailed, lashing out at whoever passed within range. And as was expected some nights were worse than others.

"Three of our lovely ladies are cracking up already tonight!" Marian sang out as Val closed the ward door behind her. Marian came and took her arm, a large false smile spread across her candy apple red lips. "Should be a sparkling night my dear!"

Val laughed with her and the two skipped arm in arm to the nurses' station to check in. Curran Ryland, charge nurse, looked frazzled and desperate, a sea of paperwork spread out in front of her. Her red hair stuck out at odd angles and her glasses had slid to the tip of her nose where they clung perilously.

"Well my girls, looks like it's going to be a long night," she sighed. "Meds have been given but something tells me at least two of our charges may be wearing a camisole before the night is through."

Val scanned the second shift incident list and saw that one of the older patients had managed to slap Esme across the face at dinner. "How is Esme?"

Nurse Ryland looked up at Val Causing her glasses to teeter and drop. "The little lamb is fine. She's cozied up in her room with a book of fairy stories one of the male orderlies fetched from the library."

"Good. And I see Sylvia is headed for a night in restraints." Val turned to see the remains of a shattered wooden chair in the day room. "You're right. We're in for it tonight."

"The natives are certainly restless. It must be a full moon." Nurse Ryland chuckled, restoring her glasses to the bridge of her nose.

Marian pinched Val's elbow and rolled her eyes with a giggle as she headed down the hall to do room checks. Val put the incident log back on the counter and went to check on Esme. She found the girl on her bed, wrapped in a cocoon of sheets and blankets, the fairy book open on her knees. Esme raised her head to see who had come to visit her, her face lighting up when she realized it was Val.

She sat on the edge of Esme's bed and patted her tiny hand. "How are you my dear? I heard you got quite the wallop today."

Esme nodded somberly.

"I know you feel bad but it wasn't your fault. Her mind is sick and she has a hard time behaving."

Esme nodded again and smiled at Val, wiggling farther down into bed, her signal for Val to tuck her in, but footsteps sounded down the hall. Esme bolted upright, closing her book, watching the door intently. Val stood and poked her head out to see Dr. Willard striding down the hall towards Esme's room and when she glanced back the child's face had clouded and she had pushed herself as far back in her bed as she could.

"Esmeralda my queen!" Willard strode into the room and sat on her bed right where Val had been sitting moments ago. "Have you been good?"

Esme nodded warily, her arms wrapped around her tiny frame until she was almost able to touch her shoulder blades. Val watched Esme as she observed their interaction; Esme was not comfortable with Dr. Willard and met his questions with her usual silence but there was a harder edge to her refusal to speak.

"I was just tucking her in Dr. Willard. It's past her bedtime."

Robert turned and looked at Val, having not realized that she was in the room. "So it is Miss Martin." He patted the empty sheets that kept Esme separate from him and rose to leave.

Val waited until he was out of sight, then tucked Esme back in, watching her relax, her eyelids beginning to droop. Edging quietly out of the room, Val stood in the hallway watching the night finally take over the ward. The main hallway lights were out, the only glow from the emergency lights and from the nurses' station. She realized too late that Dr. Willard had been waiting outside Esme's room; she started to move away but Willard was too fast.

The doctor grabbed Val by the elbow, ready to say something, when a scream split the air. Val pulled away from Dr. Willard and took off down the hall where Marian and Nurse Ryland were attempting to calm one of the women who was flailing and howling on the floor like an injured animal. The two women had just managed to wrestle the woman into a hold when Val reached them and she could see now that it was Patricia and she was covered in blood that was flowing from her battered wrists.

"How in the hell did she manage this?" Marian shrieked, trying to keep Patricia from kicking her.

"I don't know!" Nurse Rylan yelled in return, struggling to be heard over Patricia's screaming and weeping. "She needs a sedative. Immediately. Page Dr. Willard!"

The doctor came tearing around the corner, syringe in hand. "I'm here! I'm here!" He dropped to his knees and thrust the needle into Patricia's shoulder. She struggled for a moment more but she was no match for the Haldol coursing through her veins and they were able to carry her back to her room. Val joined Marian in the nurses' station and leaned against the counter as Marian reached down and pulled out two bottles of Coke, handing one to Val.

"Thanks. How'd you manage to get these?"

Marian winked at Val. "I have my ways."

Val laughed, knowing that Marian did indeed have her ways and often it was best not to ask questions, especially since the doctors' lounge was the only place that had bottles of pop.

"What was Herr Willard doing on the ward?" Marian asked, looking sideways at Val.

"Honestly, I'm not sure but he made a beeline for Esme."

"My butt he's obsessed with that girl," Marian said, shaking her head. "He comes to see her almost every night, even when he's not on call."

"That's odd. Why would he do that?"

"Oh I'm sure he just has a soft spot for her," Marian said, though she didn't sound convinced.

Val narrowed her eyes, Esme's reaction to the doctor still burning in her brain. "I suppose that makes sense."

"Yes I suppose."

They both polished off their sodas and tossed the bottles in the trash can under the desk.

"I do suppose indeed."

CHAPTER 8

One Friday afternoon, Valerie decided to wander the halls of the Haskell Building on her lunch hour. She pretended she was just sightseeing but in truth she was hoping she might find a portion of the archives and she didn't have to go far to find them; the archives happened to be in the same basement hallway, not four doors down from the records room. Seated behind an old metal desk was a shockingly young man wearing a shirt and bowtie reading, of all things, an issue of The New Yorker. Valerie reached up and knocked lightly. The man looked up and pushed his black plastic glasses up his nose, yet still squinted to be able to see Valerie clearly.

"Can I help you?"

Valerie smiled gently. "I hope so. My name is Valerie Martin, I work for the department but I used to work here."

He stared blankly and Valerie wondered if he was even listening to her, but then he sat forward and drummed his fingers on the desktop. "We have quite a chunk of archives here. I assume that's what you're looking for?" Raising his eyebrows, he motioned for Valerie to sit in the tattered brown chair in the corner of the room, then watched as she dragged it close enough to his desk that her knees bumped the cold metal.

"I'm Gene Wilkins." Gene thrust his hand over his desk without standing up from his chair. Valerie gladly shook it and nodded her head at the socially awkward young man. "What is it you're looking for?"

That was the million dollar question. "I'm not entirely certain. How are the records organized?"

"They're all by year," he said, pointing to a metal shelf lined with archival quality linen boxes, each marked with a two year span. Valerie was surprised to see that they were marked by such short time spans, assuming there wouldn't be enough information to fill so many boxes yet here it all was.

"I guess I'd like to start in 1959 when I arrived and work my way forward." She frowned and looked down at her hands. "Though I suppose that would take far too long and far too much of your time as you'd have to babysit me."

"You work here in Haskell?"

Valerie nodded.

"Then all I need is a photocopy of your ID and a signature. You can have free reign. As long as my door is open, you can have access to the archives."

"Really? That easy?"

Gene nodded, smiling. "And if you can figure out what it is you're searching for, I can try to help narrow it down. We're still in the process of computerizing all of the documents in this room but I know this collection inside and out."

"The Rain Man of NSH archives." Valerie laughed when Gene looked confused. "Never mind. It's a movie."

"Ok. I'll take your word for it. Would you like to take a look at the first box while you're here?"

She wondered if she had time to peruse a few pieces before she had to be back. Then again it wasn't like she was punching a clock or anything. She could always stay a bit later.

"Actually I would love to." She watched as Gene unfolded himself from his chair and pulled a sign-in book from the end of the shelf, then slid the first box off and set it on a work table, flipping the top open exposing sheaves of yellowed, crinkled edges. "Here, just sign here and I'll take your ID."

Valerie handed over her ID and signed her name in the book, then sat in the folding chair that was tucked under the table. Reaching into the box, she gently lifted out two years of the hospital's life—newspaper articles, staff photographs, playbills from annual patient shows, and letters from the superintendent. Most of the articles were general announcements of movies playing at the state hospital theater or dates for sleigh rides, playbills and Christmas cards sent out by the administration, but nothing that might help Valerie connect any dots.

Most pieces, however, did make Valerie smile, remembering some of the shows and Sunday movies she had seen with Esme and the other women on the ward. She loved Christmas on the ward when she, Marian, and the other girls transformed the day room into a winter wonderland. Each year Marian somehow managed to bribe one of the maintenance men to drag a small fir tree up to the ward and they strung it with popcorn and old, castoff ornaments that Valerie had begged from her parents. For many years she had a set schedule around Christmas: she worked Christmas Eve so she could sit with Esme, wrapping the presents that would be tucked under the tree. It was never anything extravagant, usually necessities like soap or shampoo. Like clockwork Valerie received money from her grandparents in a card the week before the holiday so she would spend it on books, occasionally some art supplies that would inevitably wind up locked away in the nurses' station. She wouldn't be there on Christmas Day to see the women open their gifts but it didn't matter, she could feel their joy and excitement.

Christmas dinner with her parents was awkward and stiff, though much of it was one-sided. Eleanor and Walter Martin had grown used to the idea of their only daughter working at a looney bin but every time she went home Valerie felt like a fish out of water. By the late 1960's she was going home exactly three times a year: Easter, Thanksgiving, and Christmas. Eventually Easter fell by the wayside and Valerie began finding excuses to cut her Thanksgiving and Christmas visits as short as possible. When her mother got sick in the early 70's, Valerie forced herself to visit more often, though in the end, that translated out to roughly once every two weeks. Towards the end she would sit at her mother's bedside and tell her about the women at the hospital. She had no idea if her mother listened or even cared; by then Eleanor couldn't have changed the subject if she had wanted to. At her mother's funeral Valerie sat and watched the minister presiding over the mass, talking about a woman Valerie realized she hardly knew, but she wasn't bothered by it. The moment the coffin was lowered into the ground Valerie hailed a cab and went home—to the hospital.

Valerie celebrated a total of twenty New Years at Northampton State Hospital with no one to kiss, but it didn't matter as long as she was standing in the nurses' station with the girls and Nurse Ryland counting down to midnight, toasting with the bottle of champagne that Marian pinched from the doctors' party. She would always hide a second bottle that she smuggled into the dorm where a record player would materialize and the girls would drink and dance until the overnight shift could be seen stumbling out of the hospital at the first light of day, their signal to get some sleep in preparation for the first shift of the New Year. That was her family—the ward girls, the nurses, the patients. Holding a staff photo in her hand dated 1960, Valerie could just barely pick out herself and Marian in the third row, chins held high, eyes full of pride for what they had taken on. Those were the halcyon days, times when they convinced themselves that they could help, that they could be part of some kind of change. Little did they know what the future of mental health might hold.

At the back of the file box was one final article dated January 1959, mere months before Valerie arrived, and it was the announcement of Dr. Robert Willard's appointment to the medical staff at Northampton State Hospital. Valerie was surprised to learn that he had been there such a short time yet had already managed to break hearts on almost every ward while garnering one hell of a reputation. Valerie ran her thumb over the smiling photo of Dr. Willard, a professional headshot taken with his brand new white coat. She marveled at how young he looked, how open and kind. What could he have been had he kept himself in line? she wondered. He could have been a great influence in asylum medicine; Valerie had read a number of papers he had authored and had sat in the gallery at the hospital during sessions with visiting doctors and dignitaries. There was no doubt that Robert Willard was brilliant, a gifted medical man, but he was weighed down by a tremendous ego that would eventually crush him. She added the article to the pile and tucked the papers back in the box. Such a disappointment.

"Thank you very much Gene," she said, closing the box for him to put back on the shelf.

"Did you find anything?" he asked.

Valerie shook her head and shrugged. "Not yet, but I'll be back if you don't mind." Gene handed back her ID and nodded curtly.

"I'll look forward to it." He moved away and Valerie could hear him sliding the box in with its others as she walked out into the hallway, wishing she knew what on earth it was she was looking for. She sat back down in the file room and covered her face with her hands, then rubbed her eyes, feeling a headache creeping up behind them.

Staying late with a migraine blooming was not a happy circumstance but Valerie managed to plow through another full drawer of files, finding nothing remarkable. When she was finished she went up to Bill's office where she found him on his cracked leather sofa, feet up, reading The Valley Advocate. He nearly jumped out of his skin when she knocked.

"Jesus Valerie!" He sat up, the paper sliding to the floor. "What are you still doing here?"

"Sorry to scare you," she said, hovering in the doorway while Bill struggled to shove his sock feet back into his loafers. "I lost track of time."

Bill glanced up at the clock as his left foot crashed back into its shoe. "I guess so. You'll need me to let you out. The front door is locked at 6:00 and it's 7:30."

"Actually, I was wondering, do you happen to know if anyone stayed around here after the hospital closed?" Valerie sank down into the Department of Mental Health regulation chair which inevitably wobbled and would eventually make her elbows itch.

"Taking a trip down memory lane?"

"Of sorts."

Bill thought for a second. "Not many of the ward staff. There were a few cafeteria workers, farm workers who were locals to begin with, but I can't think of anyone else."

Val had a hard time hiding her disappointment. "That's too bad."

"Well if you think about it, you and I aren't far from retirement."

"Don't remind me." Valerie chuckled. "I put it off to come back. Now I'm not quite sure what I was thinking."

"I know you did and I'm sure someone somewhere appreciates that." Bill shrugged. "We were youngsters back then but most of the folks we remember retired ages ago. Some have passed away."

Val realized he was right. When she left Northampton, time had stopped for her but obviously it hadn't for everyone else. Life had gone on.

"Oh! Wait. Do you remember Miss Graham? Barbara I think her first name was. She worked in the library when we were there."

"Actually, I do remember her. She used to pull books for Esme quite often."

"Yes, yes. She's a librarian at Forbes, the town library, just down the street. Part of her job is to care for the hospital's holdings."

"What do you mean holdings?"

"After we closed for good in 1991 we went through the library and cleared it out. All the paperback novels and newer trash was boxed up and donated, but the rest of the volumes were given a home at Forbes, some of them dating back to the hospital's founding."

"I never realized there were books that old in there. Not that I had much time to visit the library."

"Tell me about it. Most days we were lucky we even had a chance to eat and sleep."

"So true. Well maybe I'll go visit Miss Graham. I wouldn't mind seeing some of those books."

"I believe they have visiting hours tomorrow but they're limited since it's Saturday."

"Something to consider I suppose." Valerie rose and headed for the door, waving over her shoulder. "Have a good night Bill."

"You too Valerie." He swung his legs up on the couch and settled back in with his paper. Valerie assumed he was still sleeping there which made her a little sad, though she supposed she couldn't throw stones going home to an empty house.

Valerie vaguely remembered Barbara Graham, the librarian at the hospital. If she had to guess, she and Miss Graham were fairly close in age and she recalled the woman being from a college town somewhere out east, near Boston. Wellesley maybe? She remembered Barbara being a kind, quiet woman with a nice smile who was generous with the patients. She used to allow Esme to reshelve the books and was fully understanding when the child would wander off, entranced by the books on flowers and the volumes of fairy stories.

Perhaps a visit to Miss Graham was in order. If nothing else, it would get her out of her own head and give her a chance to stretch her legs.

CHAPTER 9

Frost had gathered in the corners of the windowpanes and white winter sunlight reflected off the snow that coated the grass and the sidewalks. The radiators in Valerie's apartment hissed and clanged, trying to keep up with the heat seeping from the window sashes and under the doors. There were drafts everywhere in the apartment that chased across the hardwood floors. Wrapping her scarf around her neck, Val pulled a hat over her ears, buttoned herself into her coat, and grabbed her bag. As an afterthought she tossed the list of patient suicides in her purse as well.

She was surprised by how bitter the cold was as she walked down Hospital Hill towards the center of town, the Smith College athletic fields to her left a solid sheet of ice-encrusted snow, the stables shut tight with smoke billowing from chimneys; very few of Northampton's residents were out and about. At the base of the hill the road curved to the left and Forbes Library sat off to the right, diagonally across from the main Smith College campus. The library was, architecturally, one of Valerie's favorite buildings, but she had never spent much time there. Smith had a rather expansive library of its own where the girls had done their studying and where Valerie had done much of her reading and writing.

Inside the library, Valerie took a moment to wander the main floor, taking in the beautiful arches and the unending stacks of books. There was something about the smell of books that Valerie had always loved and some of the volumes were as old as the library itself which opened in 1894, not quite forty years after the state hospital. On the second floor Valerie found the

Hampshire Room for Local History and with it, Barbara Graham. She recognized the woman right away, a rather tall, well-built brunette woman with glasses and a stylish wardrobe. Looking up from her computer, Barbara stared at Valerie, recognition dawning almost immediately.

"Well, well. Valerie Martin!" She stood and came out from behind her desk, smoothing her black pinstripe skirt before reaching out to hug Valerie. "What are you doing here?"

"I came to see you actually. Bill Dunston said I might find you here."

Her mouth fell open in surprise. "Bill Dunston? So does that mean you're back at the hospital?" She settled herself back in her chair, gesturing for Valerie to sit as well.

Valerie nodded. "I am. Well, what's left of it anyway."

"I know. It's sad isn't it?"

"It is."

"I'm always so grateful that I got to keep a part of NSH with me," she said, tipping her head towards the stacks of books behind her. "I catalogued it all myself before it came here. Every important volume, right here, filed exactly as it was in the hospital library. Those are even the original shelves. You should have seen the fit I threw to get those moved here. They were just going to destroy them!"

It was incredible; the attention to detail that had gone into preserving the state hospital's library. Though Valerie's visits there had been limited to just returning the books that Esme had borrowed, looking at those same wooden stacks scarred by a hundred years' worth of use made her throat tighten. Here was a piece of NSH that looked exactly as she remembered it.

"Barbara that's incredible. I can't even imagine the amount of effort this must have taken."

The librarian snorted. "You have no idea. First I had to get the town to agree to it, and that wasn't easy let me tell you."

"Did they not want it to happen?"

"Nope. Not in the least. In fact I think they would have been better pleased if one day the entire place just disappeared into thin air. Right off the top of that hill."

Valerie didn't find that a bit surprising. In the 1980's the governor of Massachusetts had brought a lawsuit against the hospital, turning the asylum into the blackest of marks in the town's history books. The overcrowding and underfunding were exposed, the administration torn apart for their treatment of the state's mentally ill. Even though Valerie was already in Westborough by then, she followed the case closely up until the day the final patient was transferred out of NSH.

"It was a well-won battle Barbara. You should be proud."

"Oh I am," Barbara said, blushing. "The nearer we come to demolition, the happier I am that I fought for this. In a few years there will be nothing left up there but luxury housing and shops."

The thought of strangers living on that hill, oblivious to its history, made Valerie physically ill. "Won't they save anything?"

Barbara shrugged. "They probably could have at one time. There was a reuse study done by the town but that was almost ten years ago and still nothing has happened. The longer that place sits empty the harder it will be to save any of it." Valerie could tell the topic upset her.

"What do you suppose they'll do with the fountain?"

"Hopefully it will be removed and properly stored. It would be nice to see them create a park of sorts."

"I went inside a few weeks ago." Valerie admitted quietly.

"You did? What was it like?"

"Depressing," Val sighed. "Far more depressing than it was when it was filled to bursting."

"I can't bring myself to go in there even though I know people do it all the time. I don't want to see it that way."

"It doesn't look anything like we remember. It doesn't even feel like the same place.'

"It isn't. It never will be again. All we have left is our memories."

Val was comforted by the strength of Barbara's passion for the hospital; it mirrored her own and made her feel as if she had found a kindred spirit of sorts, and somehow she found herself telling Barbara everything—explaining the drudgery of her task at the Haskell Building, her confrontation with Bill. Then she pulled the folder out of her purse and shared all her suspicions, her hunches, the little nagging feeling in the back of her mind.

"Well don't you suppose a certain number of suicides are...expected?" she asked, frowning.

Valerie certainly agreed with her, but those patients who chose to end their lives were generally the hardest cases, the ones who came in with little hope of ever leaving. "The only woman on that list who even comes close to fitting any kind of suicidal 'profile' if you will is Margaret Tanner. She's the only one with a history of true suicidal ideation. The others..."

"The others were just normal girls."

Valerie nodded sadly. Barbara certainly knew how to boil things down to their essence. The others were young women, full of hormones, riding a rollercoaster of normal human emotion. Even Ashley Collins who had taken pills wasn't truly ready to die-- it was a cry for help and with the right treatment she would easily have been able to return to her regularly

84

scheduled life.

"And you haven't found anything substantial to connect these women?"

"Just their attending, Robert Willard. The girls fit a wide range of ages and diagnoses. They lived on all three wards, and all had very different backgrounds."

Barbara continued to frown, tapping the end of a pen against her chin while she considered everything Valerie had laid out for her. "Let's consider this logically. We must be missing something. Each of these women was committed between the years of 1957 and 1968. Each was attended by Robert Willard beginning in 1959, the year he-- and you- arrived at NSH. Previous to that, the attending was a visiting physician who was employed as a consultant and Robert Willard was working at an asylum in New York State."

"How do you know all this?" Valerie asked, astonished at the amount of information Barbara had at the ready.

She jerked her thumb over her shoulder at the stacks. "Annual reports are part of the collection. I spend a lot of time reading them, mostly out of curiosity."

"Why did he leave New York?"

"That wasn't covered in the annual reports unfortunately but there was talk of a scandal involving a female patient. I hear things." She shrugged. "I used to keep my lunch in the refrigerator in the doctors' lounge."

Valerie shook her head in disgust. "Why does that not surprise me?"

"Because Robert Willard would sleep with anything that had a pulse?"

Valerie erupted with laughter. "That's quite a succinct way of putting it."

"He was a cad." Barbara shrugged as if to say, and there you go.

"That he was."

Barbara reached across and turned Val's folder so she could see it. "You have notes here about the charge nurses?"

"Yes. Do you remember Curran Ryland?"

"Vaguely. Red hair? Very Irish?"

"That's the one. She was the charge nurse on B Ward. In almost every one of the girls' files Margaret noted the frequency of Dr. Willard's off-hours visits to the patients. There were similar notes from the charge nurses on the other wards, though not nearly as many as B Ward."

"They couldn't have been the only ones to notice those visits."

Marian had noticed. Valerie remembered how often her friend had remarked on Dr. Willard's presence on the ward, especially to visit Esme. "The other ward girls noticed. They just assumed he was overly fond of Esme, the way the rest of us were."

"She's the one who used to love the fairy books, right?"

"Yes, she was."

"She was also one of the suicides."

Valerie nodded.

"Wait a minute, something just occurred to me…" Barbara stood abruptly and disappeared into the stacks. She returned with a pile of books in her hand, some of which Val recognized. "I noticed some markings in a few of these books but never thought much of them until now."

They were the fairy and flower books that Esme loved so much. Barbara opened the first volume and flipped to the middle of the book where she found what she was looking for, then turned the book so Valerie could see. There were columns of neat hash marks, each labeled with numbers above that appeared to be dates, all scribbled in a loose, childish hand.

While Valerie was puzzling over the markings, Barbara disappeared again and returned with a book of calendars from each of the years marked in the book. She peered at the dates on the pages in front of Val, flipped pages in the calendar book, then scribbled some notes. "Ok it appears that each of those dates marks the beginning of a week and there are between four and seven hash marks under each date. However, there are a number of weeks missing in 1961 from roughly August until December."

Valerie snapped to attention. "August until December you said?"

"Yes. August 1961 to December 1961. Why?"

"Robert Willard went on sabbatical that year."

CHAPTER 10

Robert Willard announced his plans for sabbatical in late July of 1961. He would be traveling to Sweden to study their system of mental health care which, he said, was far superior to that of the United States. A visiting physician from Worcester State Hospital would be filling in while he was away and he hoped to return with a wealth of knowledge that would carry Northampton through the twentieth century.

"What a load of nonsense," Marian said. "He's run out of girls in the continental United States who don't already have his number so he has to start in on the Netherlands."

Val elbowed her sharply in the ribs and hushed her. Dr. Willard was addressing each shift individually and he was being quite long winded in his announcement. Valerie had lost interest quickly, concerned only with the thought that she might have a few months of peace without him haunting her every move. Grabbing a clipboard, Val prepared to hurry off in the opposite direction the moment he was done talking; she barely made it halfway down the hall when Dr. Willard stepped in front of her, blocking her way.

"What are you doing?" Val attempted to sidestep him, he moved with her. He reached out and grabbed her, and with his hand firmly on her arm, steered Val toward the linen closet. With one hand he pulled out a bloated ring of keys and deftly unlocked the door while his other hand moved from her elbow to her wrist.

"Dr. Willard, let go of me." Her teeth clenched, Val struggled against his grip but he had a white-knuckle hold on her. She looked over his shoulder, hoping for a savior, but there was no one else in sight; the other ward girls were going about their duties and the nurses' station faced away from that end of the hall which, she realized, Dr. Willard knew full well.

She contemplated calling out but her bravado had fallen away, replaced by a fear of Dr. Willard she hadn't realized previously. He muscled her into the closet and used her body to push the door shut, then rushed forward, pinning her against the cold steel, the knob digging into her spine; she fought the urge to cry out.

"Why are you avoiding me?" His breath was hot and desperate against her cheek, his eyes wild and glassy.

"Let go of me. You're hurting me."

"I don't like being ignored Miss Martin," he hissed.

"And I don't like being manhandled Dr. Willard." Val could feel her anger rising over her fear.

Slamming his fist against the door behind Valerie's head, Willard began to seethe, white bubbles of froth collecting in the corners of his mouth. "God damn it woman!" He leaned forward then and pressed his lips roughly against Val's, pushing her teeth into the soft fleshy inside of her upper lip until she could taste blood on her tongue. She struggled against him and pushed him away, then slapped him hard across the face.

Recoiling from the slap, Robert stumbled back, Val trying desperately to find the door handle in the dark but she was too slow, he too quick. Just as her fingers found the handle she felt his long, strong hands wrap around her throat, pulling her away. He spun her around and pinned her against the shelves, jamming his knee between her legs, pushing them open. Val could feel him pressing against her as his hands moved to the front of her uniform, fumbling with the buttons. His teeth smashed against hers, sending little shockwaves of pain up behind her eyes and somewhere in the back of her mind she wondered if his hands would leave bruises on her tender skin.

Robert had rucked Val's skirt up to her hips and went to work on her slip and garter, his other hand encircling her throat. Throughout the assault Val squeezed her eyes closed, tried to disconnect from what was happening, but as she felt Robert's hand touch the warm flesh of her bare thigh, she felt a surge of adrenaline that carried her knee upwards, making contact with his groin. Val heard a satisfying grunt of pain issue forth as his grip loosened and she twisted away from him and bolted for the door. She yanked the handle and ripped it open, then ran down the hallway to the staff restroom that locked from inside. Wedging a chair under the knob, she backed into a stall and sat on the toilet, tucking her feet up so that if Robert came looking for her he wouldn't see her feet under the door.

When she finally unfolded herself from her perch, Val went to the cloudy mirror that hung over the fractured porcelain sink and marveled at the bruises blooming on her throat and the swelling in her lips which she pulled down to reveal ridges of angry teeth marks on the skin inside. Looking back on that night she remembered telling Nurse Ryland that she didn't feel well, leaving only two hours into her eight hour shift. She ran all the way back to the dorm, holding back tears of anger and mortification. She reached the dorm and headed directly for her room where she slammed the door and crawled into bed, fully clothed.

Valerie fell into an uneasy sleep. At shift's end Marian charged into Valerie's room and shook her awake.

"What the hell happened? You lit out of there like your tail was on fire!"

Val blinked, clearing the sleep from her eyes and sitting up, tears gathering in her eyes as she told Marian everything.

"That monster! How dare he put his hands on you!"

"He shouldn't have. I've made it very clear I don't take to his game playing," Val was fairly shaking with anger. "He may be able to fool the other girls but not me!"

It wasn't the first time Marian had seen that kind of predatory behavior from Dr. Willard but it was the first time she had heard of him dragging a girl into a linen closet and forcing himself on her. "You have to tell someone. He can't get away with that kind of behavior."

"And who would I tell?" Val protested. "Who would believe a word I said? A ward girl, slandering a doctor. Besides he's about to leave for months on end. I'd rather just let it lie."

Marian pursed her lips, glaring at Val, matronly and protective. "Valerie Martin. How can you say that? He attacked you for God's sake. What happens if you don't report him and he does the same to some other poor unsuspecting girl?"

Val shook her head and shrugged her shoulders. "I can't Marian. I can't risk my job."

"Valerie…"

"Marian, no. And that's it." Val threw back the covers and swung her feet over the edge of the bed. Shaking her head, Marian stormed out of Val's room and didn't speak to her for nearly two weeks, until one evening when she followed Val from the wards and into the dorm where Val found a number of the other girls already installed in her room. Marian closed the door behind her, trapping Val between herself and Allison Marquand who was standing just inside the room. Diana Colebrook, a girl Val knew very little about except that her parents also worked at NSH was perched on the edge of the immaculately spread up bed. Frances Miller and Tiny Tillott (no one knew her real name) sat cross-legged on the floor in front of the radiator, the window cracked so Frances could blow smoke out the window.

"What's going on?" Val turned on Marian, her fists balled at her sides.

Allison stood and joined Marian, the two shoulder to shoulder like a wall. "We're here to talk sense into you."

93

Understanding dawned and Val's jaw unhinged. "You told them?" Val shot at Marian, who shrugged as if to say, yeah so?

"You wouldn't listen to me Val so I went to them for help."

Tiny's not-so-tiny eyes met Val's and she nodded sagely. "You're not the first of Dr. Willard's victims but if you speak up, you could be the last."

Crossing her arms over her chest, Val stood her ground. "Absolutely not."

"If you don't tell, we will." Marian mirrored Val's defiant posture, squaring up to her friend as she might reach out and drag her away by the earlobe.

"Nurse Ryland noticed the bruises," Allison pointed to the collar of Val's cardigan. "She asked us if you were ok."

"You should tell her, then she can figure out how to handle it," Marian said. "You know you can trust her."

Val shook her head, frustrated at her friends' lack of compassion. "No. She'll have to tell Mrs. Korsinsky and that old battle axe will have me out on my fan tail."

"It's a chance you'll have to take." Marian held her ground and Val realized she wasn't about to budge.

"Fine. I'll tell Nurse Ryland on shift tomorrow."

"Tell me what?" Every head in the room snapped to as Curran Ryland walked through the door.

"Nurse Ryland. What are you doing in the dorms?" The girls sat up straight and Frances struggled to rid herself of her lit cigarette.

"Relax ladies. I'm off duty." Tucking a stray curl behind her ear, she stepped into the room and settled herself on the bed across from Diana. "I came to check on Miss Martin but it seems I've interrupted some sort of powwow."

Val looked down at her feet, her fingers tangled nervously behind her back.

"Miss Martin," she said, sighing heavily. "Let me put you out of your misery. I'm fairly certain I know exactly where those bruises came from." She held up her hand as Val began to protest. "I saw him come out of the linen closet after you took off for the ladies'. I wasn't born yesterday."

"I'm sorry."

"Sorry for what child?" Nurse Ryland was tired; they could tell—her brogue got thicker as she grew more tired. "It wasn't any of your doing. And you aren't the first my dear."

"We know," Marian said, her voice dripping with disgust. "What do we do about it?"

Nurse Ryland sighed heavily. "Nothing."

"What do you mean nothing?" Frances shrieked.

"I mean nothing will be done about it. The last girl to consider making a complaint met with nothing but trouble until the moment she handed in her resignation."

"So that's it?" Marian's cheeks were crimson with rage. "We stand by and say nothing? Do nothing?"

"No. We band together and protect our own."

"How are we supposed to do that?"

Nurse Ryland smiled slyly. "We watch that man like a hawk. One day girls, one day he will slip and do something that violates the hospital's statutes in a way that can't be defended. And when he finally does slip…there will be no one there to break his fall."

CHAPTER 11

Staring at the mounting coincidences piled in front of them, Valerie wondered if she had made the right decision in not speaking up about Dr. Willard's behavior. "Do you suppose these marks have something to do with his late night visits do you?" she asked Barbara.

"I wish I could say no, but that's my first thought. The only connection in this entire pile is that man, and here's what seems to be a log of some sort of recurring behavior kept by one of the patients whose name happens to be on that list of suicides. It's difficult to ignore."

"I hardly want to imagine what he could have been doing." Valerie put her head in her hands, and sighed. "What have I stumbled on?"

Barbara shook her head sadly. "I believe you've stumbled on something far more sinister than one could ever expect."

Valerie turned it all over in her head, wondering how to put it all together. "I think Esme was terrified of him."

"What do you mean?" Barbara asked. "What makes you say that?"

"Esme was shy, it took a lot for her to warm up to adults and it was easy to spot her favorites. Dr. Willard on the other hand—she would shrink, physically retreat from him when he came around."

"So we now have a patient who was obviously leery of a doctor who also has a reputation for being, shall we say kindly, inappropriate with the ward staff and who knows who else." Barbara sat back in her chair and put her fingers to her temples as if her head hurt. "The dates seem to coincide with Willard's movements but that could be coincidence, although a strong one. His extra visits could mean nothing except that he was concerned for his patients, but I have a hard time accepting that at this juncture."

"I have been trying to convince myself for weeks that I'm overreacting but the coincidence is just too great."

"Have you shared this with anyone else?"

Valerie shook her head. "No. First, I have nothing but a handful of coincidence and conjecture. Second, who would I tell? The hospital administration has dissolved and there's no one left but you, me, and Bill. No one else would even remember these women."

"Maybe you should talk to Bill about it. He may know who to go to."

"I haven't got enough to bring to anyone who does anything important in the department. All I have is a gut feeling that something isn't quite right with their deaths and a few dates that may or may not coincide with a licensed physician's visits to his patients." Shaking her head again, Val sighed in frustration. "No one ever reported Dr. Willard for anything, his record is spotless. Sometimes I think maybe I'm just looking for something that isn't there."

Barbara shrugged. "In any other situation I might agree with you but after everything you've told me…"

Suddenly a buzzing noise broke the silence and a gentle voice filled the library. "Thank you for visiting Forbes Library. We will be closing in fifteen minutes."

"I've wasted your entire day." Valerie gathered up her papers and tucked them back in her bag, then helped Barbara collect the pile of books they had spread over her desk so they could reshelve them. Sliding the fairy books back in place made her sad, as if she had momentarily found a piece of herself that had been missing for so long, only to have to leave it behind once again. Seeing Esme's handwriting in those books reminded Valerie that caring for Esme was the closest she had ever come to having a child of her own.

Leaving Barbara to finish her closing chores, Valerie walked slowly back up the hill. As the street began to rise sharply, she stopped and looked up at Hospital Hill, staring hard at the Kirkbride that seemed to hold her gaze and challenge her; to what she wasn't sure, but she felt as if those decaying walls were slowly breaking down their secrets, preparing them to be buried alongside the ghosts. She looked off to the left at the Memorial Complex, the tuberculosis ward that was added in the 1950's on the opposite side of the street. A for sale sign stuck out of the snow in front of the old welcome center but Valerie couldn't imagine why anyone would want to buy those stone husks. Turning back to her right Valerie took the old path that ran in front of the doctors' houses, the narrow, steep sidewalk that curved around and led back to Old Main. She ducked under the branches and headed up the hill to the male nurses' ward next door to Haskell.

To Valerie's surprise the front door yawned open on its hinges, resting casually on the wrought iron railing that leaned listlessly against the red brick. Valerie had never been inside the male dorm and she wondered if it looked like the female dorm, but as she made for the door a group of giggling teenagers poured out and stumbled down the stairs, grabbing hold of each other as they laughed as some joke Valerie hadn't heard. They looked up and spotted her but they must have silently agreed that she wasn't a threat and they walked right past her out to the street. They were probably townies who had already explored every inch of the hospital. Maybe one or two had even looked up the hospital at the library or listened to their parents' stories about the asylum on the hill. But more likely they didn't care.

Valerie decided to keep walking; one visit to the derelict buildings was enough to last a lifetime. Instead she crossed the street and headed to her little cottage that, while she referred to it as home, still didn't feel like it. It felt temporary even as she turned the key in the lock. The only problem with that transitory feeling was that Valerie had no idea what she would do when all this was over. Where would she go? There was nowhere she could even think of and even though she had plenty of money put aside she couldn't imagine herself buying a house. She couldn't reconcile herself to setting up housekeeping just to continue living alone. It felt like an embarrassment, a woman on her own like that.

She knew she was clinging to old fashioned ideals. Barbara Graham was unmarried and owned a charming little cottage in Florence near Look Park. Still she felt like a failure in spite of having attended college, built a successful career, and earned a stellar reputation within the department. There was no one to share those successes with and now here she was flitting around like some amateur sleuth, trying to solve a decades-old mystery that, for all Valerie knew, wasn't a mystery at all.

CHAPTER 12

After his sabbatical in Sweden Dr. Willard returned to a promotion. Val was never really sure what that meant in regards to his responsibilities, but it did mean he and his wife, Julia, were invited to move into one of those cottages, right next door to the superintendent. It was an honor, to be invited to live on campus. Because the girls had so deftly kept their secrets, Dr. Willard's dalliances with the staff hadn't reached the ears of the administration, or anyone else for that matter.

It wasn't long before Dr. Willard was strutting through the wards, touring them like some sort of returning deity and bestowing greetings on his loyal subjects, staff and patients alike. The moment she heard his voice, Val ducked into the ladies' room and waited there until she heard the clang of the ward doors locking, then she flushed and pretended to wash her hands just to keep up the pretense; she didn't want Dr. Willard to guess that she was hiding from him. She knew that Nurse Ryland and the other girls were watching his every move.

The moment Dr. Willard was off the ward, Nurse Ryland gathered the ward girls to make an announcement of her own. "First let me remind you that Dr. Willard's promotion means he will be spending more time on the wards. Keep sharp," She said, looking meaningfully at each girl. "Second, this Wednesday you will all be required to work first shift as well as your regular shift here on second to prepare for a visit from the good doctor's wife."

A collective groan traveled through the crowd but Nurse Ryland put her hand up to shush them. "I know. I don't like it either. But the man is climbing the ranks and we have been notified from on high that we are to look our best for Mrs. Willard. We are the only female ward she will be visiting and we will put a shine on our faces."

And so the ward was scrubbed clean, the tattered furniture carried to the basement and traded for brand new pieces, and artwork hung on the walls. The patients cleaned their rooms- though there wasn't much for them to do other than to scrub the floors and make their beds. On the morning of Mrs. Willard's visit, Val and the other second shifters helped the women scrub their faces and change into new dresses that had been brought in from the staff's personal wardrobes. Val had brought in scraps of pink ribbon and carefully braided Esme's long black hair into neat plaits that fell to the middle of her back, tied at the ends with perfect little bows. They hustled all the women out into the day room and readied them to greet Julia Willard.

Val and the other ward girls stood behind the patients, one staff member to each lady, ready to spring into action should one of them forget her manners in front of the doctor's wife. The ward doors opened and Mrs. Willard was ushered in on her husband's arm, accompanied by the superintendent, Dr. Steinman; the ward superintendent, Mr. Phillips; and the head physician, Dr. Fitzgerald. She wore a simple burgundy shirt dress that buttoned down the front and fell below her knees with a cardigan draped over her shoulders and held in place at her throat with a pearl chain clip. Her low-heeled white shoes were likely chosen for their semblance to the rubber soled shoes the ward girls wore, though of course Mrs. Willard's were far more stylish.

Dr. Steinman tried his best to introduce the staff to Mrs. Willard but since he rarely left his office in Old Main, he had a difficult time recalling most of the names, resulting in the staff members stepping forward to introduce themselves. Mrs. Willard shook each hand that was proffered and smiled warmly as the ward girls introduced each patient. She hovered over Esme, then crouched down to look at the little girl's face.

"You must be Esme. My husband talks of nothing but you." Mrs. Willard had a heavy German accent, her voice low and deep, like melted chocolate. Esme shrunk behind Val while Mrs. Willard inspected her. "Your hair is so beautiful."

Esme reached back to take Val's hand, her safety blanket. "She doesn't speak Mrs. Willard."

Julia straightened and turned her gaze to Valerie who had draped an arm protectively over Esme's shoulder, still holding her hand. "You must be Valerie Martin. I've heard quite a bit about you as well."

Val felt her smile falter but kept it in place. "It's a pleasure to meet you ma'am."

"Please, call me Julia. I hear you are an invaluable asset on this ward. You have a way with the women."

So, her husband had held his tongue in front of his wife. Val nodded ever so slightly, relieved that Julia Willard seemed to have no inkling of Val's encounters with her husband.

"Thank you ma'am."

Mrs. Willard nodded. "Of course."

Val thought she saw something in Mrs. Willard's eye, a spark of...well, she didn't know what of. She wondered how much Mrs. Willard knew of her husband's dalliances, or how he treated women; perhaps more than she had assumed. Val raised her chin a fraction under the woman's withering gaze, hoping she conveyed to Mrs. Willard that she was different from the others.

Julia Willard continued to look carefully at Valerie as if she was measuring her, sussing her out and testing her weight in her head. Was this woman someone to be trusted, or was she like the others?

"Do you have children of your own Miss Martin?"

"No ma'am. I'm not married."

"Please, call me Julia," she purred again, reaching out to touch Val's elbow as she spoke.

It seemed Val had passed some kind of silent test; Julia had decided she was not a threat. "I apologize for putting you on the spot. I'd like to talk with you more Miss Martin."

Val nodded, wondering if Mrs. Willard just wanted to keep an eye on her, likely keeping her at arm's length but well within reach. Mrs. Willard continued down the line, greeting the women by name, shaking the hands of the ward staff. Mrs. Korsinsky stood at attention, Nurse Ryland at her side, but Val could tell they were both pleased. When Mrs. Willard finally departed a sigh of relief rippled through the ward, staff and patients alike. The women scattered, some settling in to enjoy the sunlight streaming into the day room, others shuttled to therapy groups or other activities. Mrs. Korsinsky motioned for the second shift girls to gather around her and lowered her voice conspiratorially.

"I want you all to clear out and meet me in the day room of the dorm," she said, rubbing her hands together. "Don't you dare, any of you, be late. That's an order!"

Marian grabbed Val's arm and raised her eyebrows, whispering in her ear, "If it wasn't for her smile I would think we were on our way to a tongue lashing."

Giggling, Val fell into step with Marian and out into the summer air. It was August and the heat was in full force, but Val was enjoying the feel of the sun on her face and arms. By the time they reached the ward both girls were damp with sweat, their uniforms sticking to their skin. They went in the front door, rather than the side, and into the first floor day room where they found a buffet table, laden with food, a bucket filled with ice and bottles of Coke, trays of cakes and cookies. Mrs. Korsinsky clapped her hands to get everyone's attention, Nurse Ryland at her elbow.

"Well ladies, I have to say, you were all shining stars today. I believe Mrs. Willard was very impressed by the presentation we put forth." She and Nurse Ryland began to clap their hands, nodding appreciatively at each of the girls as they joined in the applause. "Thank you all for your hard work and for making Mrs. Willard feel welcome. I want you all to enjoy a nice, leisurely meal and a bit of fun. As we speak the maintenance staff are setting up sprinklers on the lawn outside the dorm."

A cheer rose up amongst the girls, a few rushing to the windows to watch the setup. Mrs. Korsinsky stepped forward and began helping to serve the food while some of the girls worked to drag chairs out to the grass. Others ran to their rooms to grab blankets and towels to sit on while Marian and Val piled their plates high before joining Allison and Lily on a blanket out in the sun.

"Well this is a lovely way to pass an afternoon," Allison said as she popped a chocolate chip cookie in her mouth.

"We'll all be going back to the ward this evening with sunburns." Marian was already lying on her stomach, the skirt of her uniform hiked up above her knees.

Val sighed comfortably and sipped her Coke, watching the girls who were already clad in bathing suits, tripping happily through the sprinklers. "We earned it ladies. And we'll walk on shift tonight full of good food and good fun."

Much to everyone's surprise, that first visit to the ward was not to be Mrs. Willard's last. It appeared that she was taking her role as doctor's wife seriously, visiting first shift twice more that month. As August rolled into September, Valerie heard the other girls talking about Julia's visits. They said that Mrs. Willard read to Esme every day and attended arts and crafts with some of the older women. In spite of herself, Val was impressed by the woman's dedication, but of course she believed it was all for show; until the day Nurse Ryland handed her an envelope.

"What's this?"

Nurse Ryland shrugged. "It came for you this morning."

Vale turned the envelope over but it hadn't come by mail- it had no postmark, only her name. It had come from within the hospital.

"Looks fancy," Nurse Ryland remarked. It did at that; the stock was heavy, the envelope lined. Val ran her fingers over the paper's nap, nervous to open it but her curiosity got the better of her as she grabbed a letter opener out of the desk and slit the envelope from corner to corner.

"It's an invitation." Val tipped the card so that Curran could see it. It was handwritten, embossed initials at the top. "From Mrs. Willard. She wants me to come for tea."

"Who even has 'tea' anymore?" Marian had snuck up behind Val and was reading over her shoulder.

"No one but the queen." Nurse Ryland drawled in her best Irish brogue.

"And Mrs. Willard apparently." Val shook her head, laughing. "I can't imagine what she wants."

Marian snorted. "She wants to interrogate you."

"No she doesn't." But in the back of her mind Val knew that was the case and it made her dread sitting down with Mrs. Willard, not that she had a choice.

CHAPTER 13

Had anyone asked her then, Val would have been hard pressed to say that tea with Mrs. Willard would be one of the most pleasant afternoons she had ever spent in another woman's company; thirty years later she was fairly certain that invitation was still packed away somewhere amongst her belongings. As nervous as she was about being alone with Julia Willard, Val also knew that Mrs. Willard could prove to be a very valuable connection and in the end that first meeting set the stage for a very unlikely alliance.

Val chose her best summer dress, carefully pinning her hair back and pinching her cheeks until they glowed. The invite was for a 1:00 tea and Mrs. Willard promised to be done bending Val's ear in plenty of time for her to change before shift. Val wandered across the lawns in front of Old Main to the smallest of the cottages where Julia had laid out a lovely silver tea service on a wicker patio set.

"I wanted to have tea outside because it's absolutely sweltering in the cottage." Val noticed that Julia's voice was much more relaxed and her accent a bit thicker than it had been on the ward.

"Thank you. It's beautiful out here." Val sat across from Mrs. Willard and looked out at the fountain burbling away just in front of the portico. The cottages were close to the road but the backyards faced the main buildings with a sweeping view down to the Smith College fields.

"The woman who lived here previously tended a glorious garden as you can see. I'm afraid I don't have her green thumb." She sighed, a deep, very ladylike sound. "So, Miss Martin, may I call you Valerie?"

"The ward girls call me Val," she said, accepting a cup of tea from Mrs. Willard's outstretched hand.

"Val then. I have to say I've heard a great deal about you."

"All good I hope."

Mrs. Willard's laugh rang through the flower buds and drifted away down the hill. "You are too modest." She looked off into the sun and let her smile fade as she lifted her teacup to her lips but did not take a sip, as if she had forgotten where she was or what she was doing. "I didn't want to come here at first you know."

Obviously Val had not known that but she could have guessed at it. What young wife, even one in a marriage such as Julia's, wanted to be constantly moved from one insane asylum to the next, making her home within the reaches of madmen and murderers?

"I liked New York. When Robert first took the job at Binghamton I didn't quite relish living on the grounds of an asylum, but I understood that it was his work. I had just barely gotten used to it when he told me we would be coming here."

Having no idea what to say to this confession, Val sipped her own tea and remained silent.

"You must think me ungrateful, full of myself perhaps," Julia said, her eyes fixed on the hospital. "It wasn't easy, moving yet again, living amongst the patients and adjusting to yet another set of rules and expectations, but here we are and now my husband has been promoted." She gestured at the peeling white clapboards of the cottage and smiled. "I have my own home now, which is splendid and now Robert is looking ahead to Dr. Fitzgerald's retirement. He is hoping the position will be his."

Valerie continued to nod, still not certain what this had to do with her.

"As his wife I have decided to do more with my time than simply organize functions and attend luncheons. I would like to help my husband affect change, especially for the women in this institution."

"That's quite a noble goal." Val hoped she didn't sound patronizing but she was having a hard time figuring out what her responsibility might be in all this.

"It's a nightmare if I'm being honest."

Val was shocked at her candor. "How so?"

"It's mostly to do with funding, but quite a bit of it is also a clash between medical and psychiatric staff." She shifted in her chair and crossed her legs, folding her hands over her knee having discarded now empty teacup. "My husband has been doing battle for ages with the medical staff, fighting with them over proper treatment for the patients."

"You mean like the women who are painfully overmedicated?" The words were out of her mouth before Val even had time to consider her impertinence and she raised hand to her lips as if she could simply tuck the words back in, but instead of being horrified, Julia laughed.

"Please, don't feel you have to censor yourself. You're absolutely right about the medication. That's a large part of it. But there's more to it, like basic human rights. The medical staff treat these patients like wild captives, a pack of dogs sent to them for the sole purpose of discovering the next medical achievement like they are Pavlov or something." It came out sounding like "somesink".

Once she got over the shock of Mrs. Willard's openness, Val took in what she was saying and nodded in agreement. Though she generally tried to let it all roll off her back, there were so many times when she had a difficult time agreeing with and upholding hospital policies. She found it especially upsetting when women would come to Northampton State Hospital, suitcase in hand, packed with some of their most treasured belongings, and it was taken away to storage. The administration firmly believed that it was imperative to separate patients from reminders of their past but Val often wondered how these women could possibly heal when they spent all their time missing the things they loved most.

"I'm not sure there's much that can be done about those things." Val knew that many of the hospital's practices had been set in stone for more than a hundred years. What made this woman, of all people, think she could change it now?

"I know a lot of these beliefs are deep-seated but you should see how they do it in Sweden." She went off on a tangent about the things she and Robert had observed abroad, but Val wasn't listening. All the research in the world wasn't going to convince these doctors that the women weren't cattle to be treated however they saw fit.

"Mrs. Willard..."

"Julia, please." She smiled and leaned forward to refresh Valerie's cup.

"Julia, I think first you need to acknowledge the lack of necessities on the ward." Val cleared her throat nervously, feeling as if she was mouthing off to a superior even though Julia Willard wasn't much older than she. Val told her that the women didn't have enough feminine products; staff brought them in themselves. For the entire three years that Val had worked on B Ward the girls had taken on the purchasing of Christmas gifts for the women. They decorated the ward, all out of their own pockets, spending hours stringing berries and popcorn, weaving them into the old metal trees that looked scabrous and worn. They brought in books for the patients to read because the library had no current novels or magazines. The women were not allowed access to cosmetics or even to their own hair brushes and they wore the same drab gray sackcloth dresses day after day, even though none of them fit properly.

Julia sat back in her chair and shook her head. "I feel like I should be taking notes! So the dresses the women wear when I come to visit..."

"They belong to the ward girls. We dressed them especially for you."

"Unbelievable." Julia shook her head and muttered a German curse under her breath. "So each time I visit them, what I'm seeing is a charade."

Val nodded. "Essentially. Try coming in unannounced. You'll see a whole other world."

Julia sat back and brought her elegantly polished fingertips to her chin, tapping thoughtfully. "I believe I just might."

Val returned to the ward with her head spinning. After changing into her uniform, she pulled her suitcase out from under her bed, the one she had packed the day she left Smith for Northampton State Hospital in which she had hidden some of her most important belongings. Underneath the lining of her shiny blue Samsonite was a well-worn leather bound notebook that she had gotten for Christmas from her parents; they had bought her one every year since she was old enough to hold a pen though the past two years the notebooks had come to her in care of the asylum, wrapped with boxes of chocolate covered crackers and tubes of lipstick. Her mother also sent a box of Crane Stationery and two bottles of ink; one black, one blue.

Val took the journal out of her suitcase and set it on her desk, then dug out a pen and a jar of ink. Opening the journal to the next empty page, Val made a quick bulleted list of the things he had discussed with Julia, then stopped to think about the other things she felt needed immediate attention. It was the first time in months that she had written anything in the journal—she just didn't have the time- but she didn't want to forget anything in case she had another chance to talk with Mrs. Willard.

To her surprise, Julia invited Val back a week later, then once a week every week after that. Each time they pushed their meeting an hour earlier until they began having brunch together and talking until Val was nearly late for shift. They talked about the things they envisioned for the women of the ward and Julia took the salient points back to the committee of doctors' wives who, up until Julia's reign, had remained rather passive.

Julia convinced the wives to set up a book drive and invite the town, an event that revitalized the hospital's library. She approached the top hospital donors and talked them into revamping the beauty salon so the women could have their hair set and colored. The sackcloth dresses remained but Julia instituted a reward program of sorts where the women could "earn" their personal clothing-- without belts and sashes of course. Val then helped Julia connect with Smith College to bring in volunteers who came regularly to do activities with the women. Though things were improving in the light of day, Val continually urged Julia to make a surprise visit on second shift.

Many of the dyed-in-the-wool staff who had been at NSH since the dawn of man did not believe that the changes made on B Ward were warranted. Mrs. Korsinsky firmly believed that the women did not deserve the creature comforts being provided to them and Val began to notice that the moment second shift began all the books, magazines, and art supplies were locked away in the nurses' station. Mrs. Korsinsky required the women to change into their hospital grays the moment they were done with dinner, insisting it made nighttime routines simpler. Val began mentioning it to Julia, worrying that the nurse's lousy attitude might derail all the good they had done, but

Mrs. Willard wisely said not to poke that particular bear.

By late fall, as it neared Halloween, Val and Julia began planning a pumpkin carving in the day room. Robert was always conspicuously absent from their meetings, though Val certainly wasn't complaining, and she noticed that Julia mentioned him less and less as their time together passed. However, as they discussed finding some more innocuous Jack-o-lantern faces for the women to carve, Julia blindsided Val with her first and most incendiary comment about her marriage.

"I know that Robert strays," she said quietly without looking up from the Halloween picture book in her lap. By now they had moved their meetings into the dining room of the cottage which Julia had painted royal blue with white trim, and they sat comfortably with a fire burning in the grate. Even though it was the 1960's and the height of the floral print craze, Julia's European tastes had turned the cottage into a cozy, sophisticated jewel-toned haven. "The way he talked I always assumed he had taken up with you."

Valerie was staring at Julia, watching her as she calmly flipped through pictures of pumpkins and painted gourds. The moment struck Valerie as so surreal that she burst out laughing and soon Julia had joined her, the two laughing together until tears streamed down their cheeks.

"God I'm pathetic," Julia said, wiping her eyes with the back of her hand. "I know he and I don't have a traditional marriage but he could at least try to hide his habits."

Val tried to reign in her laughter, shaking her head. "Just the idea of me and your husband…" She pretended to shudder in disgust. "I don't mean to offend you."

"No offense taken. He certainly doesn't deserve your apologies."

"Julia, I'm so sorry you have to live with that man."

She laughed again. "So am I, but at least now, with these projects you and I are working on I'm finding ways to make the best of it. I thought that helping these women would keep my mind off it all and help me to find some worth in my days."

"Well it certainly seems to be working." It was the truth as far as Val was concerned. Julia seemed happier, full of purpose. "The women are incredibly grateful you know."

"I know. They tell me whenever I come to the ward. They show off their dresses, they make me cards when they work with the Smithies. It's a wonderful feeling."

"From what I've heard, the entire culture of the first shift has changed for the better."

"Yes, but second shift is still an issue."

Val nodded. "I was hoping it wouldn't be that way but we've met with no end of pushback."

Julia wasn't happy with Mrs. Korsinsky but so far she hadn't been able to exert much pressure on the head nurse. "I too was hoping the first shift changes would carry over." She sighed. "I had visions of family style dinners and evenings around the television, the women learning to knit. Instead the patients have a day full of joy clouded by the knowledge that it will all be taken away at shift change."

"Maybe it's finally time for that unannounced visit we've been talking about."

Sitting back, Julia looked thoughtful. "You're right, maybe it is high time I popped in."

"Come this evening. The sooner the better."

"You know, I think I will." Julia peered at her watch. "It's time I let you go anyway. You need to get ready."

Valerie said goodbye to her friend at the backyard gate where she promised to ring the bell promptly at 6:30 when the women would be preparing for dinner. That night Val started doing room checks earlier than usual, hoping to be otherwise occupied when Julia showed up so no one would know she had encouraged the visit, but as she approached Esme's room, she heard Dr. Willard's voice floating out into the hallway and she realized he was there visiting Esme.

Marian was heading down the hall and Val grabbed her on the way by. "What is Dr. Willard doing here?"

Marian shrugged and rolled her eyes. "Who knows, but you can't honestly tell me you're surprised he's here. His presence is as regular as mealtime around here."

"I'm not surprised in the least, but this could be bad Marian."

"What could be bad?"

Val was about to explain the whole thing when the ward bell rang and Mrs. Korsinsky got up from her post in the nurses' station, looking puzzled.

"Who's coming on the ward this late?" Marian whispered. The docs had keys and didn't need to ring in. If someone was ringing the bell, it was an outsider at the door.

"I'll tell you later, but it would be best if you cleared out for a bit." Val broke away from Marian as Mrs. Korsinsky opened the ward doors to find Julia Willard standing there.

"Mrs. Willard. This is a surprise." Mrs. Korsinsky stood in front of Julia, blocking her view of the ward. "I'm sorry but I didn't know you were coming to visit."

"That's because I didn't announce it Mrs. Korsinsky." Mrs. Willard smiled, the curve of her lips sly, knowing; she had expected that very reaction.

"It's nearing dinner time Mrs. Willard," she said evenly, continuing to block Julia's way. "We don't allow visitors at this time of day."

There were still a few patients in the day room, the stragglers who hadn't yet been forced into their rooms to change, and they were now craning their necks, trying to see what was going on at the door. Curiosity got the better of a few them and they got up from their chairs, shuffling down the hall to rubberneck. Mrs. Korsinsky turned around, ready to admonish the patients for being up and about, then locked eyes with Val glaring at her, but Val held her ground and Mrs. Korsinsky's punishing gaze.

"Mrs. Korsinsky, let me in please," Julia commanded quietly as her smile vanished.

"I'm sorry Mrs. Willard. I can't allow that." Mrs. Korsinsky had raised her voice, an obvious attempt to intimidate Mrs. Willard into leaving but Julia simply lifted her chin a fraction higher and raised her voice to match the nurse's.

"Mrs. Korsinsky, you will step aside and allow me to inspect this ward or I will report you to Dr. Fitzgerald." She paused to let her threat sink in. "I have been granted unfettered access to these wards and I am ordering you to step aside."

As the standoff in the hallway escalated, the ward girls began to make themselves scarce, ducking into patient rooms, running to the ladies'. Val was afraid that Dr. Willard would catch wind of the ensuing cat fight between his wife and his head nurse and, not wanting him to come out and intervene-- she didn't want his two cents where her schemes with Julia were concerned-she slipped into Esme's room and eased the door shut behind her.

Robert was seated on the edge of Esme's bed while the child cowered in the corner, her blankets gathered around her and her eyes flashing wild. He was speaking quietly, too low for Val to make out exactly what he was saying but it was clear that Esme was good and frightened.

"What the hell do you think you're doing?" Val stepped out of the shadows, her hands clenched at her sides, ready to strike. Robert started; he hadn't noticed Val standing in the room and every muscle in his jaw tensed. He seemed to forget that Esme was there, watching everything as he flew off the bed and came at Val like a madman.

"You little whore!" His hands were out and on Valerie's throat before she could even put up her fists to defend herself. He gained such a hold on her throat that try as she might she couldn't free herself. She tried to wedge her fingers between his hands and her windpipe, then tried to twist out of his grip but he was too angry and too strong. The only option she had was to kick out and hope that she connected with something tender.

With a sudden cry Esme was out of her bed and on Dr. Willard's shoulders, her tiny fingers clawing at his face and his eyes. His elbow shot back, knocking her to the floor and loosening his grip just enough to allow Val to twist out of his hands and wrench open the door where both Mrs. Korsinsky and Mrs. Willard were standing just outside the room.

Willard came crashing out into the hallway, spittle flying from his lips, pointing as Esme who was crumpled on the floor, sobbing. "That child attacked me!" he bellowed as Val fell to the floor and gathered Esme in her arms, rocking her and trying to calm her.

"Robert?" Julia stepped in front of her husband, snapping her fingers in front of him to get his attention. "What are you doing here? What happened?"

Willard looked stunned to see his wife standing before him. "Julia. I was...I was following up with a patient and stopped to check on the child. She was agitated earlier and I thought she was calmed but then she attacked me."

"She was provoked," Val said over the wails of Esme's tears.

"Shut up!" he yelled, raising his hand as if to strike Val, then thinking better of it. "Get that child in restraints!" he bellowed at Mrs. Korsinsky.

Willard stormed past the women and down the hallway. The next sound they heard was the slamming of the ward door as he left and Mrs. Korsinsky motioned for Val to help her lift Esme from the floor but she refused to move. Mrs. Korsinsky shook her head and leaned out the door to yell for Marian as Julia stared at Val, her eyes traveling down to the bruises blooming on Val's throat. Marian came running into the room and helped Mrs. Korsinsky wrestle Esme onto her bed where leather restraints were pulled out from under the mattress. Marian glanced at Val over her shoulder as Mrs. Korsinsky tightened the leather cuffs onto Esme's limbs. Val shook her head sadly, tears streaming down her cheeks as the child continued to sob wordlessly and suddenly Val needed desperately to get out of the room; there was nothing more she could do to help Esme.

Julia was hot on her heels and followed Val through the ward door-- which Robert had failed to lock- and out into the main hallway. "What the hell happened in there?"

Val had no words. She couldn't think of a way to tell her friend that her monster of a husband had just tried to strangle her. Instead she just shook her head and thumbed tears away from her eyes.

"He attacked you. I can see thumbprints on your throat." Julia rested her hand on Val's shoulder. "I'm so sorry. I know he has a temper."

Valerie looked up at Julia, disgusted. "That's all you have to say? He has a temper?" She pulled away and rang the ward bell. They heard the lock tumble and Mrs. Korsinsky appeared. "Mrs. Willard, it's time for you to be leaving." She turned to Val, fire in her eyes. "As for you, stay away from that child. Don't go in her room for any reason."

"I need to check on her."

"No you don't." Mrs. Korsinsky stepped out of the shadows and reached out to touch Val's throat. "She doesn't need to see those bruises. She's calm now and that will just scare her all over again." Dropping her hand back to her side she reached for her keys and ushered Val into the nurses' station. "Get an ice pack out of the freezer. You'll remain in here for the rest of your shift." She pointed to the little anteroom where the nurses did their reports; it was hidden from view by a row of filing cabinets. Her expression turned hard. "I expect you to cover those bruises before you come back on shift."

Val nodded and allowed Mrs. Korsinsky to guide her into the next room. "Oh, and Miss Martin?" Val turned and saw that whatever kindness Mrs. Korsinsky might have earlier possessed had been erased. "We'll hear nothing more of this. And we will never have another unannounced visit from Mrs.

Willard. Am I understood?"

Nodding, Val turned and walked away, the bruises on her throat beginning to throb.

CHAPTER 14

Reports of suicides in asylums rarely made it to the papers. Going through the archives Valerie hardly expected to find any mention of Esme's death because as deeply as it had affected her, it had caused barely a ripple in the hospital's grand façade. Still Valerie hoped to find something significant in those sterile boxes, something that might tell her she was wrong to believe those girls were murdered, but the papers she had sifted through so far were neither here nor there. Every so often Gene would sidle up to her and peer over her shoulder, then disappear back to his desk. It took her a couple of weeks but she managed to look at every piece of paper retained between 1959 and 1989 where the file ended with Robert Willard's obituary. He was survived by a younger sister who lived in Arizona with her husband and three children; his parents had passed when he was in medical school. As she read his obituary she began to wonder.

"Gene, I have a question for you." She handed him Robert's obituary and waited while he perused it. "Can you find out more about this man for me?"

"Who is he?"

"Someone I worked with many years ago."

Gene shrugged and turned to his computer. "Sure. What are you looking for?"

Valerie considered just what it was she was hoping to find. "I'd like to know more about his life before he came to Northampton."

"Ok. Here goes nothing." Gene typed Robert Willard's name into his computer and waited while it made laborious whirring and clicking noises. After a few minutes a list of sorts popped up on the screen and he gestured for Valerie to come around and take a look. "These are all the times that Dr. Robert Willard has been mentioned in a public document. I used his title to narrow it down but if you want I can take away the doctor part but it'll get you hundreds of results."

"No that's ok. I'll start here. May I?" Valerie gestured at his chair and Gene scooted back but didn't get up. She sighed, grabbed the folding chair, and pulled it up to the desk where she began to read. Halfway down the page something caught her eye. "This one," she said, pointing to a newspaper headline. "How do I see the rest of this?"

Gene pushed Valerie aside and clicked on the headline, opening up another screen. "I have to request it from the main archives in Waltham."

"How long will it take?"

Gene looked up at the clock and frowned. "We missed today's pickup but I could put the request in the mail tomorrow. If it gets pulled right away it could be here by the end of the week."

Valerie tried hard to hide her disappointment; she knew Gene was doing his best to help.

"Ok I guess I'll have to be patient."

"I'll give you a heads up when it gets here," Gene said, giving Valerie a half-hearted smile.

Happily Gene was right and a photocopy of the article arrived in Friday morning's mail. He came to find her in the records room and handed her the envelope almost reverently.

"It just came," he said, shifting from foot to foot, waiting for her to open it though she wasn't quite sure she wanted to in front of him. Then again, at this point, what harm could it do now?

Valerie slid her finger under the lip of the envelope and broke the seal, sliding the article out and laying it on the table. She could feel Gene hovering over her shoulder, his breathing quick and excited as he scanned the headline along with her.

"Suspicious death at New York State asylum for the insane." She heard him suck in his breath as he began to read aloud.

"The New York State Office of Mental Health has received a report of a suspicious death at Binghamton State Hospital. The patient's name has not yet been released pending notification of next of kin but hospital administrators have confirmed the patient was a female found dead in her room. The death has been ruled suspicious after doctors confirmed the presence of high levels of secobarbital in her blood." Gene stopped reading and furrowed his brow. "Why would that be suspicious? Isn't that just seconol, a sleeping medication?"

"Yes, but in high doses it can also be used to euthanize a human being."

Esme's death forced Dr. Willard to keep his distance from the ward. An investigation was opened which required the attending to be temporarily removed from the ward and all activity suspended; the Smith girls were notified and promises made that they would be contacted when their visits would be allowed to resume—Val was grateful for the respite from the outside world so she could grieve in private. The investigation was concluded quickly and Esme's death ruled, without question, a suicide. The child had remained in restraints, chained to the metal bed in her room for three days. Val was off the night they removed Esme's restraints, but Marian had told her everything.

Esme had been brought her dinner in her room after the others had eaten then Marian had read her a story from the volume of fairy tales she loved so much, then tucked her in. No one heard a sound from her room and somehow she had gotten skipped over on the first round of bed checks. They didn't find her until shortly after midnight and they tried to cut her down as quickly as they could but it was too late. Esme had no family so there had been no funeral; she was buried under a numbered stone in the hospital cemetery, her room emptied.

Mrs. Korsinsky took advantage of the situation and returned the ward to its previous status quo, leaving the women to brood in solitary silence, their moods as gray as their dresses. Val said nothing—she no longer had the energy to fight, she no longer wanted change. Her zeal for change, her push for Julia to visit the ward had led to Esme's death. That was enough change to last a lifetime as far as Val was concerned.

By the time Dr. Willard was allowed to return to the ward Val's bruises had faded, as had her friendship with Julia. In spite of the woman's blunt assessment of her husband's faults, Val knew that their bond would not survive all that had happened. It was too much. She saw Julia in passing, often as she was leaving the ward at the end of first shift; sometimes she only caught sight of Mrs. Willard in the garden of the little cottage venting her frustrations at the browning plants and wilting flowers. Val did not actually hear from her until almost a year later when, instead of sending an invitation to the cottage, Julia showed up at the dorm, knocking on Val's door as she sat reading in front of the window.

Val looked up, surprised to see the woman standing there, large sunglasses perched on her nose and a wide brimmed hat on her head. "Julia. What are you doing here?"

"I need to talk. Can I come in?"

Val nodded and stood, offering Julia her chair, then taking a seat on the edge of the bed. Julia removed her glasses and Val gasped at the sight of the bruise ringing her right eye and crawling down her cheek. "Oh my God Julia! Did Robert do that to you?" Val stood and reached out to tilt Julia's face to the light but she pulled away.

"No. I fell and hit my head on the bureau," she said quietly.

Val shook her head. "I don't believe you."

"You're not meant to." She sighed and brought her hands to her forehead. "But that will be my story should anyone else ask."

"I wish I had something strong to offer you."

Julia shook her head and waved away Val's concern. "Things just keep getting worse with him. Far worse since Esme's death. He snapped when that little girl died and he started drinking."

"And exercising his temper obviously." Val felt anger and disgust welling up inside her. It was one thing for him to attack her, a ward girl who could get away from him. It was another to batter his wife who could not get away, would have no place to go to hide from him. "What are you going to do?"

Laughing ruefully, Julia hung her head. "What can I do? I'm not a native of this country. My husband is a respected psychiatrist. When he did this," she pointed to her eye. "He said that if I reported my injuries he would make certain that I found myself on C Ward by day's end."

"He told you he'd have you committed? To the violent ward?"

"He said he would claim I attacked him in a fury and he feared for his life. He would put a kitchen knife in my hand and make it look as if I tried to kill him. Even though it was quite the opposite."

What consolation could Val possibly offer? Dr. Willard was wily, a practiced liar, and no one had reason to contradict him; no one knew his reputation.

"He would ruin me," Julia sighed, tears collecting in the corners of her eyes.

"You're right. He would." There was nothing left to say, no way to advise her. Back then, to leave your husband and accuse him of laying his hands on you just wasn't done. Julia's circumstances further complicated the situation and were far too tenuous to test by speaking out.

Julia stayed in Val's room until it was time for shift change and though she didn't say much else, she did say she was sorry she hadn't spoken up that night in Esme's room. Val said she understood, though she doubly regretted her choice to remain silent, knowing that Robert was now victimizing his wife. After that, the two women tried to revive their friendship, slowly at first; Val wondered what Dr. Willard might think if he knew Val and Julia were speaking again, but if he was aware he didn't let on.

Eventually the other women on the ward—staff and patients alike- stopped mentioning Esme and one day in late summer of 1969, a new patient was given the child's room. Mrs. Korsinsky said it had been empty long enough to exorcise the demons; but not the ones that cast a darkness in Val's heart. Julia saw how Val struggled to get through her days and eventually talked her into applying for a ward supervisor position on A Ward where she could get away and try to forget. It was a first shift position with an increase in pay, and Julia put in a word for her, but Val didn't really care about all that. She cared only that the attending physician was not Dr. Willard but an older, gentler man named Dr. Muirhead. The head nurse on A Ward was a woman about Val's age who had noticed the changes Val had helped usher onto B Ward and was interested in doing the same for her own charges.

The women on A Ward never stayed long; most of them were there for a "rest" or to get away from the stresses of everyday life. Some were even there voluntarily and frequently received visitors. It didn't take long to institute the same changes on A Ward as they had on B, though Marian said B Ward never did get back to good. The Smith girls began coming to A Ward instead, often leading off grounds trips and organizing movies in the hospital's auditorium. They took the women bowling and ice skating, even swimming at the Smith College pool. Val on the other hand kept her distance.

There had been a time when Val had seriously considered finding a way to take Esme in when her time at NSH came to an end. She had grown so attached to the little girl that she thought perhaps she could make a home for them both and try to give Esme the love that might help her to find her voice again. Instead Val's fierce attachment to the child had led to her death.

In the end, Val stayed on A Ward for the remainder of her time at Northampton State Hospital, hearing less and less of Mrs. Willard until the late 1970's when Valerie heard through the grapevine that Julia had divorced the good doctor. In 1990 she received a beautifully engraved invitation in the mail, her last from Julia, inviting Val to her wedding. She was engaged to a German man, a carpenter who had done work on the cottage at the hospital; Val did not attend the wedding. After the divorce, Dr. Willard was passed over for that promotion he had so desperately desired and by 1989 he was dead.

He hadn't deserved to die the way he did, broken and alone at the foot of his grand staircase but now that Valerie had amassed this mountain of evidence it was obvious to her that Dr. Willard's temper had widened its net, ensnaring not only his wife, but his patients as well. The more she dwelled on it, the stronger the conclusion she arrived at: Robert Willard was a murderer.

CHAPTER 15

"So it's definitely Willard." Barbara leaned back in her chair and crossed her arms over her chest while Valerie sat across from her with a cup of tea in her hand, the newspaper article spread out on Barbara's desk. Valerie had filled Barbara in on Willard's history of violence, including his volatile marriage, though she only hinted at his behavior with her; she wasn't quite ready to open that Pandora's Box just yet.

"I'm starting to think so, yes." Valerie sipped her tea and sighed. "I had my suspicions in the beginning but now, at this point, I can't argue the evidence against him."

Barbara shook her head in astonishment. "It certainly is damning."

The library was busy that Saturday, full of children who were there with their mothers for a reading of a popular children's book. They buzzed in and out of the stacks but Barbara's haven was separated from the main library floor by a glass door; it was like watching a silent movie. Valerie turned to look out the small window above Barbara's desk, the only one in the room so that the antique volumes would not be damaged by excess sunlight. She watched the clouds scud across the sky and wondered what to do with it all.

"Maybe now is the time to bring this to Bill," she said, looking imploringly at Valerie. "I think it's imperative that someone else knows besides the two of us. It's too much to carry."

Val nodded absently. She dreaded rehashing all this with Bill. He already hated Robert Willard and this would just cement his poor opinion of the man. And how would he feel about Valerie when he found out that she could have come forward years ago and perhaps save a number of patients from meeting a grisly end at Willard's hands, yet chose to protect her own hide instead?

Of course she knew Barbara was right. In the simplest terms, Valerie had once prided herself on the level of care she provided for the women on her ward, but if she continued to keep this secret, she would be a hypocrite. It was the right of every woman, of every person who passed through Northampton State Hospital over its roughly one hundred year existence, to be laid to rest comfortably, her family certain of her fate. For many of those women, their families may well have spent decades shunning their memory for committing the mortal sin of ending her life when in fact that wife, mother, daughter had had her life taken rudely from her by another human being.
But could she bring herself to ruin a man in that way, no matter what she suspected Robert Willard had been capable of? Then again if he was, as they assumed, guilty then he brought it on himself, ruining his own legacy the moment he decided to take advantage of the human beings who were mistakenly put in his care. Valerie also worried deeply that exposing Willard would undo all the good things they had done at the hospital. There was a chance that once the murders became public that this would be the thing everyone talked about, destroying any hope that NSH had of living on in fond memories.

Already people were so eager to see the hospital demolished and replaced by luxury housing that no one would be able to afford. The hospital was already a blight on the town of Northampton, a dark chapter of the past that most residents would prefer to forget. Most of the old guard, the keepers of those pleasantries, were either long dead or on the cusp of retiring. Soon there would be no one left who could even tell what the inside of an asylum looked like let alone what it felt like, smelled like, sounded like. Photographs would be the only thing to survive and already most of those were locked away in state archives, none of them accessible to the public. For however long the asylum remained standing it would simply be the haunted castle at the top of the hill that kids dared each other to go inside, nothing more.

It was a depressing thought that Northampton State Hospital would soon morph into a distant stream of smoke-filled dreams that only Valerie would have; the generations of patients who called the hospital home would disappear, just as their gravestones had in the cemetery. She knew it would take courage to lay it all out for Bill, courage she had lacked thirty years ago when she should have come forward. Of course from her vantage point here, thirty years later, it was easy to say what she should have done, could have done, but in the end she hadn't. Now was the time to make it right.

CHAPTER 16

Valerie gathered up every piece of evidence she had amassed—the tally of suicides, copies of the pages of the fairy books, the newspaper article. She had spent days coming up with just the right words to explain what she and Barbara had come up with, including her reasons why she hadn't reported Dr. Willard when she had the chance. Valerie hoped that Bill would understand her confusion and her fear; after all, Dr. Willard had made it clear how dangerous he could truly be, and not just physically. He had threatened Julia with commitment and there had been no reason for Valerie to doubt that he wouldn't do the same to her if she had gone over his head. No, she thought, there was no way anyone could fault her for keeping quiet.

She knocked on Bill's door with a trembling hand, ready to tell him everything she had found, everything that she and Barbara had worked out with a little help from Gene and his archives.

"Bill?" He looked up from the stack of forms on his desk and smiled, but it faded at the sight of Valerie's ashen face.

"Valerie, what's wrong? You're white as a sheet."

"Bill, I have something I need to talk to you about."

"Oh god, you're not quitting are you?" He pushed back from his desk and scraped his hands down his face. "Shit. I knew that job was too much for one person. I told the Department it was too much. Ok. Well, you gave it your best."

Valerie waved her hand to get Bill's attention. "No Bill, I'm not quitting. I'll finish the job, but first I need to show you something." She handed him the folder and let him flip through it.

Bill opened the folder and quickly scanned the contents. "Valerie, what am I looking at?"

"It's something I found when I was going through the files. It started months ago but the puzzle just finally came together."

"It's a count of suicides on B and C Wards during Robert Willard's tenure." Valerie cleared her throat. "Suspicious suicides. I found them when I was going through the files."

"When?"

"When?" Valerie had hoped he wouldn't ask that. "Actually I found the first one months ago but the puzzle just finally came together."

Bill raised his eyebrows but went back to the papers in the folder, picking up the article from the New York paper. As he began to read, Valerie sank into the leather couch under the window and let her thoughts drift until she heard Bill close the folder and drop it on his desk.

"God damn it Valerie. Why didn't you come to me with this sooner?"

Valerie hung her head and explained that she hadn't been certain what she had discovered until she and Barbara found the fairy and flower books Esme had loved "We wanted to be certain."

"And you didn't think you could tell me the truth that he had attacked you?" Bill's voice was softer now, the angry edge tempered by something that almost resembled sadness. "All those times I harangued you about him and you could have just told me what a bastard he really was."

"Honestly Bill, I was ashamed. I allowed myself to be swayed by the others. They told me it was better to keep quiet, that reporting him would only lead to problems so I didn't and Esme died because I didn't come forward. It was my fault but by then it was too late so instead I left the ward."

Bill sighed and pulled off his glasses, throwing them down on top of the folder. "So now it seems that Robert Willard was not only a philandering dirt bag, but also a murderer. I'm going to have to notify the department."

"That's what I was afraid of," Valerie said, dropping her head in her hands. "What's going to happen to me when they realize I could have stopped him all those years ago and I didn't?"

"You can't think that way Valerie." Bill stood and came around to sit next to her on the couch. He put his hand on her shoulder and squeezed. "There's nothing you or anyone else could have done to stop him." The others had been right-- no one would have listened to a woman who was accusing a handsome, wealthy doctor of being a predator of women. They probably would have told her to be flattered and continue on with her job.

"It sounds so terrible when you say it out loud like that."

Bill said he would take care of notifying the Department of Mental Health and there would most certainly be an investigation but Bill would be with her every step of the way. They would of course want a statement and then they would have to confirm everything Valerie had discovered but that would be on them, not her.

"I can't even imagine the can of worms this will open." Valerie sighed. "Will they have to exhume these women?"

"I would assume so," Bill said, leaning back into the arm of the couch. "There would have to be a medical inquest to prove that the deaths weren't suicide."

"That chemical they found in that woman's system in New York, would it show up after all these years?"

Bill wasn't sure and neither was Valerie, but someone in the department would know. They had experts on their payroll.

Valerie stayed on the couch while Bill made the call. The conversation was brief and to the point, Bill refusing to go into detail over the phone. When he hung up he told Valerie that the department's legal team was being dispatched and would arrive from Boston the next day. Until then, they wanted her activity in the file room suspended which was to be expected.

"In the meantime, you might want to let Barbara know what's happening and keep her in the loop, just in case she gets pulled into this."

"This is going to be a nightmare." Valerie picked up the phone and dialed the library but Barbara didn't pick up.

"It is. I'm going to go make sure the file room looks presentable, even though I'm sure you left it spic and span." Bill headed for the door. "And Valerie?"

"Yes?"

"I'm sorry you had to carry this with you."

"So am I Bill. So am I."

CHAPTER 17

As she put the key in the front door of the cottage, Valerie could hear the phone ringing inside and she rushed to pick it up, hoping it was Barbara.

"Hello?"

"Valerie?"

There was something very familiar about the female voice on the other end of the phone though she couldn't immediately place it. "Yes, this is Valerie."

"Valerie, it's Julia."

Valerie pulled the phone away from her ear and stared at it for a moment, then regained her voice. "Julia? How did you find me?"

"I called your office in Westborough. They said you had gone back to Northampton." On the other end of the phone, Julia exhaled like she had just taken a drag on a cigarette. Valerie wondered when it was she had taken up smoking. Maybe after Robert had died.

"I got back a few months ago. They needed me to go through some files."

The conversation stalled momentarily. Julia obviously hadn't decided on what she wanted to say and Valerie was trying to find a polite way to ask her why she was calling out of the blue for the first time in more than ten years.

"I got your wedding invitation. Sorry I couldn't make it. I had already moved." She had no idea why she had just blurted that out.

"It's ok. I figured as much." Julia paused to exhale again. "Listen Val, I called for a reason. I know it's been a while."

"Yeah it has. About twelve years to be exact."

Silence. "How is it to be back?"

"It's strange Julia. Very strange."

"My husband died."

"I know. I heard."

Julia sighed heavily. "No, I mean my second husband. He died. Last week. I didn't know who else to call."

"Oh Julia, I'm so sorry."

"I didn't know who else to call," she said again and began to cry quietly. Valerie waited for her to get it all out before making comforting noises into the phone.

"Where are you living now?"

Julia sniffled. "I'm still in Florence. I was hoping we could have coffee or something."

Coffee? Was she serious? Valerie sighed. "Of course. When did you want to meet?"

"Tonight?"

Julia sounded so sad and desperate that Valerie found it impossible to wiggle out of it. "How about 7:30 at the Hotel Northampton?"

"That sounds good Val." She took one last drag on her cigarette, not even attempting to exhale away from the phone this time. "Thank you."

Valerie hung up the phone and just stood there, leaning against the kitchen counter, hoping it was just coincidence that Julia had called. There didn't seem much chance that she knew what was happening but she wondered what Julia might think of her husband being accused of murder. She likely wouldn't be surprised. Valerie turned away to put the kettle on and as she waited for it to boil as the phone rang again. This time it was Barbara.

"What's going on?"

"I told Bill everything." She recounted her conversation with Bill, though there wasn't much to tell and Barbara was not at all surprised by Bill's level-headed reaction to the whole story. "The department has been notified and their attorneys will be here tomorrow."

"Pff...wow." Barbara had been holding her breath as Valerie spoke. "That's going to be quite the event."

Valerie poured a cup of tea and made the bag dance in the cup, turning the water a rich golden brown. "You have no idea. And then, get this, Julia Willard called."

"What?! How did she even find you?"

"She says she called my office in Westborough and they told her I had come back to Northampton." Valerie replayed their conversation in her head. "Actually, she never explained how she got my number after that."

"Why is she calling you after all these years? It's been what, ten years?"

"Twelve."

Twelve years. Aside from the wedding invitation she had ignored, Valerie hadn't heard from Julia in twelve years. Whatever bond they had forged while on the wards dissolved in the face of Robert's violence, taking their friendship with it.

"That's a hell of a coincidence that she called you the day Bill notified the department of her ex-husband's possible murdering tendencies. Did she say what she wanted?"

"She said her husband died. Her second husband, the German man she married after Robert. She wants to get coffee tonight."

"Are you going to go?"

"I told her I would."

Barb pulled the phone away and coughed. "But you're not sure you want to."

It was less a question than a statement. "No, I'm not sure at all."

"Well, look at it this way. You were once close to her and though she didn't come forward, she didn't have anything to do with Dr. Willard's behavior. She was a victim."

And she had been Valerie's friend. Regardless of what Robert had done, Valerie and Julia had been friends, real friends. They had been almost as close as Valerie had been with Marian, in fact when she thought about it, she actually knew more about Julia than she did about Marian.

"Hear her out. See what she has to say."

Julia Willard was quite a mystery, the unluckiest woman Valerie had ever known. Julia hadn't married for love—she had married for safety which, in the end, turned out to be a bitter kind of irony, but of course Julia never could have predicted that her husband would turn out to be almost as dangerous as Hitler's SS. Julia waved to Valerie from her seat inside the coffee house and Valerie hesitated slightly. Could she sit across from Julia and not tell her what was going on?

Her first thought was that the years had not been kind to Julia Willard. Her skin was rutted and wrinkled, lines crowding the corners of her eyes and mouth, a permanent crease perched between her brows. She may have claimed to be happier in her second marriage but Valerie could see in her eyes that her station had not been much improved.

"What is it really like being back?" Julia barely looked up from her tea, pushing the remains of a raspberry scone around her plate. It had taken her close to twenty minutes of small talk to get around to asking about the hospital.

"It's taxing, remembering it all." Remembering that your husband was a monster.

"I haven't thought about that place in years but Gerhardt wanted his ashes scattered near the woodshed. That's why I called." She sighed. "The memories."

"You were scattering your husband's ashes and that's what made you think to call me?" She knew she was being nasty but she couldn't help it. Julia was a fool to think that the two of them could sit and chat normally after all the time that had passed.

"Val," she said, reaching across the table and touching Valerie's arm; she fought the urge to pull away. "You know what I mean. The hospital made me think of you."

Valerie carefully disengaged herself from Julia's fingertips and gazed out the window. The street lights were on and had been since 5:00 when the winter dusk had descended. The cold had thinned the crowds though Valerie could still see a line gathering outside the Academy of Music, brave souls anxious

147

to buy tickets to whatever happened to be on stage.

"Julia, what do you really want?" Valerie turned and caught Julia's eye, holding her gaze steady. Julia flinched and looked away.

"I don't really know anymore Val." She turned back, toying with the spoon in her cup. "We used to be friends, didn't we? I remember I could tell you just about anything."

Valerie was suddenly wary of Julia, thinking she heard a subtle message coming through loud and clear. Julia was wondering if Valerie had kept her secrets, especially now that Valerie was back at Northampton—and Julia wasn't. It dawned on her that Julia was concerned her reputation—or her ex-husband's- might have been tarnished.

"What is it that you're fishing for, exactly?" Valerie took a sip of her tea, assessing Julia over the rim of her mug. "I've never told anyone what I know."

"Haven't you? I stopped at Forbes Library when I got back in town. I wanted to see the hospital collection. Imagine my surprise when I saw you talking to that librarian. Your voice carries you know."

"And that's why you called. You heard me tell Barbara that Robert hit you."

The anger crept into her cheeks, her thin fingers balled into fists under the table. "You told her everything. I told you that in confidence."

"It's no longer just about you Julia." Valerie fished a handful of ones out of her wallet and tossed them on the table, then stood to go.

"What is that supposed to mean?" Julia grabbed Valerie's wrist and held her fast.

Yanking her arm from Julia's grip, Valerie walked out and left Julia sitting at the table, dumbfounded and furious. Robert's behavior with his wife was an essential piece of the puzzle and Julia's feelings couldn't be taken into consideration at this point. It was everyone else's feelings and opinions that had stopped Valerie from reporting him in the first place so she could say with a clean conscience that she had broken that confidence for a greater good.

CHAPTER 18

Nerves settled like concrete in Valerie's stomach and she skipped breakfast that morning. Not knowing what to expect from the meeting was taking a toll, greater than if she had known for certain she was headed for the gallows. She met Bill in his office, noticing that he looked just as worn and nervous as she was.

"Morning Valerie. Are you ready for the Spanish Inquisition?"

Valerie shook her head and dragged off her coat, hanging it on the coat rack near the door. "Not in the least."

"Do you want to go over it all one more time before the sharks arrive?"

"No. It's burned into my brain. I won't have any problem telling them what I know."

Bill pressed his lips together, then nodded. He clearly wanted to review the information but Valerie didn't think she could bring herself to talk about it more than was absolutely necessary. It was going to be hard enough to go over it once with complete strangers; reviewing it first would just sap her of the energy she needed to keep it together. They sat together on the couch waiting for the attorneys to show up, Bill polishing off cup after cup of coffee while Valerie shifted around on the couch, unable to sit still. Finally a group of black suits appeared in the doorway, then seeped into Bill's office.

"Mr. Dunston. Thank you for having us."

As if they had been given a choice. "Thank you for coming so quickly gentleman," Bill stood and gestured to the chairs scattered around his office.

The man who had greeted Bill turned his attention to Valerie and approached to shake her hand. She stood and gripped his hand firmly trying to maintain eye contact. "Miss Martin. How are you?"

"As well as can be expected under the circumstances, thank you."

"You don't remember me do you?" He smiled brightly and laughed.

Valerie looked closely at the man. His face wasn't familiar but his eyes were, and somewhere in the back of her mind, she recognized his voice too. "I do, but I can't place you."

"Lawrence Porter. Larry. I came to Northampton at the same time as Mr. Dunston here."

"Oh yes!" Valerie felt her shoulders loosen. One of the apocalyptic horsemen had been a ward orderly, just like her. "I do remember you. My God. Whatever happened to you?"

Larry chuckled. "Well I ended up on C Ward of all places. I was fresh out of the Army and they thought I would be able to handle the more...difficult...patients. Then Vietnam started..."

One of the other attorneys cleared his throat and Larry stopped himself from reminiscing. "We can talk more later. Let's get started."

For three hours Valerie rehashed everything she had found, everything she remembered from her time on the wards, and every detail she knew about the women who had died. Occasionally Bill would interrupt to clarify a particular bit of information or to move the questioning along, but he mostly stayed silent, watching Valerie to be certain she was handling it all well enough. When the tide of questions finally receded, Valerie sat back and took a deep breath, her chest deflating from the final divestment of her secrets.

"Well Miss Martin we appreciate you going through all of this," Mr. Porter said, making eye contact for the first time since she had started speaking. "As you can imagine we will have to open an official investigation." The department investigators would be in contact frequently while Larry would be staying behind to personally oversee the proceedings in Northampton.

Bill nodded and stood. "I thank you gentlemen for coming and getting this out of the way so quickly. I assume you want access to the records room?"

"Yes, but not today." Larry shook Bill's hand, then Valerie's, nodding goodbye. "I would prefer if you continued to keep the file room closed and untouched."

"Of course, though you may want Valerie's help when it comes time to go through them. She knows that file room well."

Larry nodded at Valerie for a second time, offering her a shy smile. "That goes without saying. Thank you again Miss Martin."

Valerie watched them depart then turned to Bill. "Well, that went swimmingly."

Bill stood with his arms crossed, frowning. "I'm not so sure about that. I was watching their reactions as you were talking and some of them definitely didn't believe what you were saying."

"I don't need them all to believe me. Just one is enough." And she had a feeling that Larry Porter believed her. "I'm going to head home. Let me know if and when you need me."

Valerie grabbed her things and walked outside where the bitter cold hit her like a wall. The forecast was calling for more snow just in time for Thanksgiving which was only days away. Barbara had invited her to eat at her house with her family, an invitation that Valerie was seriously considering accepting as she hadn't had a proper Thanksgiving meal in years and it would be nice to feel like part of a family even if it was someone else's, and even if it was for just one day.

Chapel Street was quiet; it was the middle of the day and all her neighbors were still at work. Valerie hated being home during working hours and though she knew it was an irrational thought, she felt as if she was being punished for something even though she knew the work stoppage was temporary. It made her feel useless, a feeling she truly hated so she decided to tamp down those feelings by cleaning the cottage from top to bottom. At some point in the afternoon her phone rang but she let the machine pick it up then turned off the ringer. She didn't have the energy to talk to anyone just yet, not even Barbara, so she left her messages for later. Once the cottage was spotless Valerie sat down to read but instead drifted off to sleep, a paperback book spread out on her chest. When she opened her eyes again it was dark outside and her answering machine was blinking furiously.

Reluctantly she got up and played the messages, two of which were from Barbara checking in, asking her how it had gone with the attorneys and one from Bill telling her that she needed to come in the next morning but not until 9:00, which was when Mr. Porter would be ready to begin sifting through the files. The final message was from Mr. Porter himself.

"Miss Martin, I wanted to say that it was lovely seeing you this morning in spite of the circumstances. Regardless, I'm looking forward to seeing you again." He cleared his throat, then there was a clattering sound as he hung up the phone.

Standing over the machine, Valerie realized she was happy he had called. Hearing his voice had momentarily calmed her nerves and reminded her that though they were dealing with a very serious situation, he was still a human being and would be there with her through the course of the investigation. It also sparked a tightening in her chest that she hadn't felt in many years.

Valerie remembered the day Larry and Bill had come to NSH as Mrs. Korsinsky led the two young men around the ward, and though nearly three decades had passed, she also recalled thinking that Larry Porter was a very attractive man. He hadn't seemed at all daunted by his surroundings, unlike Bill who jumped like a spooked cat at every noise. Even Esme had watched Mr. Porter carefully and with curiosity and Valerie had wondered which, if either of them, would be back on the ward. She had been more than slightly disappointed when the young man with the green eyes and the warm smile hadn't returned.

It was obvious Mr. Porter had done well for himself, climbing the ranks within the department and it was nice to see a somewhat familiar face in the midst of the turmoil, but that could not relieve her stress entirely and she spent the night tossing and turning. Morning came slowly and Valerie woke to a ringing phone at 7:00 am. She picked it up, expecting it to be Bill but instead it was Mr. Porter on the line.

"Miss Martin. I hope I didn't wake you."

"No, not at all." Valerie wiped her eyes and yawned, leaning her forehead against the wall next to the receiver. "What can I do for you?"

"I'd like to take a preliminary look through the records. Would you be able to join me?"

"Yes of course. Bill actually called yesterday to say you'd be looking for me around 9:00."

"Is that ok? I'll bring coffee."

Valerie smiled. "Sounds good."

She hung up and took an extra-long shower, trying to wash away the exhaustion that had settled into her bones. It was going to be a long day so she dressed neatly yet comfortably, pulling her hair back and tucking her feet into her boots. Valerie walked up Chapel Street and crossed to the Haskell Building where Mr. Porter was waiting for her in the lobby.

"Mr. Porter. Nice to see you again." She held out her hand to shake his, a firm handshake at that.

"Larry, please."

Valerie nodded. "Larry then. Shall we?" she said, holding the door for him. "The records room is this way."

He followed her down to the basement where Bill was ready to unlock the records room. "Morning all."

"Morning." Larry nodded to Bill, then followed Valerie into the rows of file cabinets.

"I'll leave you to it then. I'll be in my office if you need me." Bill bowed out, pulling the door closed behind him.

"Where do you need to start?" Valerie asked as the door clicked shut.

"Well, why don't you show me the first file you found and we'll work from there?"

Valerie walked over to the cabinets and pulled open the drawer that held Ashley's file. "She walked him through each suicide, pulling the folders out one at a time, then stopping at Esme's. "Esme was the first to raise alarm bells. She was a patient on the wards in the early 1960's and I knew her well, very well." She swallowed the lump in her throat and kept going. "There were similarities between her file and Ashley Collins' which is what prompted me to keep digging."

She moved slowly through the timetable, pausing only occasionally to answer a question or two from Larry who was taking copious notes. He wrote down names, dates, and little details she would not have otherwise assumed to be important. They worked through the files carefully, the pile in front of them growing until it began to lean precariously and slide across the table.

"What made you suspect Willard, besides the fact that these girls were all his patients?"

"Well, to be honest, he was…aggressive. And that night in Esme's room his reaction was way out of line." Valerie looked down at her hands, then back up at Larry. "He beat his wife too." She shook her head sadly. "He had a hell of a temper."

"You know this for a fact?"

"Yes," Val nodded. "Julia—his wife- and I were friends once. She came to me the first time he put his hands on her, and I had plenty of my own run-ins with him."

Larry nodded as if he knew exactly what Valerie was talking about but she knew he was a decent man who couldn't possibly imagine someone like Willard trying to crush her windpipe in front of a mentally ill child. "What happened to his wife?"

"She divorced him finally, remarried a couple years later. Funny enough, she called me the other day."

"That's some interesting timing."

"Exactly what I was thinking."

Larry frowned. "What did she want?"

"She wanted to have coffee with me." Valerie recounted her entire conversation with Julia including her little blowup. In spite of everything she had found, Valerie wondered aloud if she had made a mistake in breaking Julia's confidence, though she still thought Julia's anger was way out of proportion for the situation.

"Can I ask you something?" Larry tapped his pen on the pad of paper in front of him. "Are you certain that Julia's story is true?"

"What do you mean?"

Larry brought the pen down and tapped his chin with it, looking thoughtful for a moment and carefully collecting his words. "Hear me out. You said Julia's anger at your sharing her secret was fairly intense which to me, sounds slightly out of line with the seriousness, or lack thereof, of what you shared." He sat forward, on a roll now. "Her ex-husband is long dead, his reputation largely in tatters already. Why would she go nuclear thirty years later just because she heard you tell Barbara about her marital problems? It makes me wonder how much truth there is to her story."

"But I saw the bruises."

Larry shrugged. "That doesn't mean Dr. Willard was responsible."

"Are you suggesting she did it to herself?" Valerie couldn't believe what she was hearing.

"It's possible. You say she was aware of her husband's infidelity and told you she was more than unhappy about her circumstances. Maybe she saw an opportunity. A way out."

Valerie considered it but had a hard time imagining Julia giving herself a black eye. "So you think she swore me to secrecy hoping I would do the opposite, that I would somehow help her take him down?"

Larry shrugged again. "That may very well be."

Valerie never would have thought Julia capable of that high a level of manipulation but then Larry's theory certainly was plausible—she had seen an opportunity to break away from a man who had cheated on her and largely ignored her. If she could make him out to be some sort of habitual abuser without directly pointing the finger at him...

"He wouldn't be able to have her committed."

"What?"

Valerie slapped her hand on the table as the pieces clicked together. "It all makes sense now. I would bet that her story about Willard threatening to have her committed was true, it just happened under different circumstances." Julia must have threatened to leave him not because he had hit her, but because of his cheating. A divorce would have ruined his career so he threatened her with the only ammunition he had: locking her up and throwing away the key. It would be far easier to explain away a mentally ill wife than a messy, public divorce.

"Mr. Porter, I do believe you may be onto something."

CHAPTER 19

They called it quits after that; Larry had at least ten pages of notes and Valerie's head was buzzing. "I'm sure I don't have to tell you this, but this investigation is not public knowledge," Larry said, locking the file room behind him.

Obviously he meant Julia. "Of course."

Larry opened the door and started to walk away, then turned back to Valerie. "Do you have plans for dinner?"

Valerie looked up, surprised. "No, not usually."

"Well, how would you feel about joining me at Hotel Northampton? I could pick you up around 8:00?"

She wanted to play it cool, at least pretend to think about his invitation but instead she blurted, "Yes. Yes, that would be fine."

Valerie felt the heat of embarrassment creep into her cheeks and the tips of her ears which she hid by wrapping her scarf around her face as she followed Larry out the front door. He smiled, waved and watched him walk out to the parking lot where he climbed into a battered rental car, an old Ford.

The last two days had made her feel restless and drained, yet jittery and overwrought at the same time. It was times like these when she wished she had someone to talk to; a husband, friends, her parents. Shortly after her mother passed, Valerie's father packed up the house that he and his wife had called home for nearly fifty years and moved to an assisted living center that reminded Valerie of the morgue at NSH. She would visit her father one Sunday each month and watch the elderly borders shuffle aimlessly through their days, her father now confined to a wheelchair and beginning to lose his faculties. When he stopped recognizing Valerie, she stopped visiting and made arrangements for the nursing home to contact her if he took a turn for the worse.

Aside from her affections for her patients, Valerie was quiet with her emotions. Even as a teenager she hadn't been like the other girls, publicly forming and discarding crushes on the boys at school on an almost hourly basis. She had instead focused on her studies, was editor of the school paper, and joined the cheerleading squad and not because she suffered from a surfeit of cheer, but because it would look good on her transcript. Her acceptance to Smith had been her ticket out of her staid, wealthy hometown of Amherst, and though Smith was only minutes down Route 9, Valerie had insisted on living on campus and the moment she opened the door to her dorm room she felt like she had crossed into a whole other world.

Though not marrying hadn't initially been a conscious decision, it would take the passing of years to make Valerie think about what life would be like this far down the road. She had watched numerous college girlfriends, and later her coworkers, find someone, settle down, and get married. Valerie allowed ambition to replace romance and once she became a ward supervisor she got a taste for advancement her focus shifting away from patient care and onto hospital policy and improvement. Did she regret never marrying? At times like these, a bit. She wished she had a partner, someone to carry some of the burden of simply living, but she harbored no romantic notions.

Valerie had just finished unpinning her hair and smoothing it into waves when her doorbell rang. She glanced at her watch as she opened the door; it was 7:40.

"I'm sorry, I'm early," Larry apologized, pointing to his own watch. "It's funny, I've been in Boston for so long I forget that it doesn't take forty-five minutes to get everywhere in Western Mass."

Valerie smiled and waved away his concern. "Not a problem. I just finished getting ready." Climbing into the passenger seat of his rental, she took a minute to look closely at the grown up Larry Porter. He still had the same wavy brown hair and green eyes but with the addition of a neat goatee and mustache. He was still tall and lean but his features were softly aged, the lines around his eyes inviting. He was a good looking man and he still carried himself with a slight military bearing. Valerie realized that her palms were damp and she had butterflies in her gut. She was nervous; no, not nervous. Giddy, girlish even, though this dinner with Larry was just casual. He had asked her because he was in a strange town with no one else for company. At least that's what she was going to tell herself.

"So how has it been, being back?"

"Huh?" Valerie had been so deep in thought she hadn't realized he was talking to her.

"Northampton. Has it changed much?"

Valerie shrugged. "In a million ways, but then again, not at all." It was strange but true. It looked different, and sounded different, but somehow it all felt exactly the same.

"I agree," he said, pulling away from the curb and heading down the hill. "The moment I got back here it felt as if I never left even though I didn't have nearly as much time here as you did."

"It's strange how this place does that." Valerie looked past Larry at the hospital as it crawled by. "Nothing looks the same anymore but it's still home."

They passed the rest of the ride in comfortable silence, the car's heater hissing and popping as it blew out lukewarm air; it was a good thing it wasn't nearly as cold as it had been that past week. Larry pulled into a space behind the hotel and led her into the Coolidge Park Cafe, one of the restaurants inside the Northampton. It was quiet, elegant yet casual, and Valerie immediately fell in love with it. They sat near a window overlooking King Street and gazed out into the crowds just as new flakes of snow began to fall.

"I didn't realize it was supposed to snow."

Larry watched the specks of white float to the ground. "Neither did I, but it certainly makes for quite a scene out there." He turned and looked around the restaurant. "It also seems to have scared away quite a few people."

"We certainly do have the place to ourselves," Valerie said, pulling her chair closer to the table.

"So how are you feeling in the aftermath of our conversation about Mrs. Willard?" Larry tapped his fingertips against his water glass.

Valerie snorted. "You know, I feel like I should be at least the tiniest bit shocked by the idea that Julia Willard might be a bit more devious than I expected but I have to say it makes a whole lot of sense."

"It's scary, isn't it," Larry said, sucking air through his teeth as if he'd just gotten pinched in the arm. "It's a punch to the gut to think that a friend could have tried to use you like that."

"It certainly is. But at the same time, I don't feel bad. I kept her secret so whatever evil plan she had in store didn't work. It would have been all over the hospital if it had."

As a waiter approached to take their order, Larry leaned back in his chair and looked thoughtful. "What was Robert Willard's reputation exactly? I've heard a number of different stories but I'd like to hear your take."

Valerie gave the waiter her order, then considered for a moment, looking down at her hands clasped on the table. "Robert Willard was brilliant. Or so he thought. I think he was just the squeaky wheel to be honest."

"What do you mean?"

Robert was always going around telling everyone how wonderful he was; no one ever really arrived at that conclusion on their own. He preached to everyone who would listen, many who had no interest at all but would tell him he was a genius just to get him to stop talking. Essentially he was his own biggest fan, an egomaniac when it came not only to medicine, but also to women.

Sighing, Larry shook his head and chuckled. "Trust me, I've heard the stories. Some of them fairly appalling. I always wondered how he got away with what he did and yet somehow managed to not only have a job, but to wrangle promotions on top of that."

"He did a fair job of hiding what he was from those who mattered. You have to remember, the administrators who were responsible for his fate at that hospital were rarely, if ever, on the floor. They never spoke to the rest of us so they were easily kept in the dark. The only reports they received about Willard were those he himself had approved."

Speaking this frankly about Robert Willard wasn't easy but she felt that Larry was being very open-minded about the whole thing. He wasn't making any snap judgements or taking sides, though it would have been easy for him to dismiss Valerie as hysterical or hyper imaginative. Instead he kept her talking and validated all of her feelings and all of her fears. He seemed to understand that this was all real for her.

"Sometimes I have a hard time believing that this is what my life has become." She sighed as the waiter placed their dinners in front of them, and she asked for another glass of wine to help dull the edges and keep her talking. "I wonder what people who have never worked at a state hospital would think of all of our stories. I can't imagine trying to tell someone outside of the field what I've done, what I've seen."

Larry agreed, adding that he also couldn't imagine trying to talk about his day with his spouse, explaining what he did every day. "Oh yes, it was lovely dear. I had a patient try to choke me today but we gave him Thorazine and within minutes he was a drooling mess." He laughed. "It doesn't exactly translate, does it?"

"No, you're right. It doesn't." But she could certainly imagine coming home and telling someone like Larry how her day was. And not just because he would understand everything she told him. "It gets lonely sometimes though."

She wasn't sure what had possessed her to say that out loud but Larry nodded in agreement. "That it does. I assume that means you've never been married?"

"I haven't. Have you?"

He shook his head, smiling sadly. "No. I haven't."

"Well, aren't we a sad lot." Val laughed.

"Indeed."

They chatted amiably and finished their dinners. Together they polished off half a dozen glasses of wine and whether it was the alcohol, the company, or a combination of both, Valerie found herself laughing more than she had in quite some time.

"You know, I had a crush on you from the moment I laid eyes on you all those years ago." Larry was looking at her, running his fingers around the rim of his half empty wine glass.

Valerie had been daydreaming, staring into her own glass, and looked up, wondering if she had heard him wrong. "What?"

"It's true," he laughed, shrugging his shoulders. "I wanted to find a way to call on you but I didn't end up on your ward. I was so disappointed."

"That makes us an even sadder lot because I also had hoped you would be on my ward." She shook her head; it had to be the wine talking. There was no way she would have admitted these things otherwise.

Larry looked at her for a moment, smiling, then said, "I think we should consider this a first date then. Thirty years in the making, but a first date nonetheless."

CHAPTER 20

A first date. Valerie had just had her first successful first date without warning. At her age, she supposed it was right that there had been no fanfare, no nervous primping, no awkward small talk. It was a first date that felt like it had been thirty years in the making.

At work, Larry continued to be a consummate professional, focused purely on concluding his investigation. He asked Valerie a million more questions and she continued to show him everything she could think of that might help make sense of things. They even combed through the files Valerie hadn't marked just to be sure nothing had been missed while Larry praised her for her thoroughness and for her keen eye; she in turn thanked him for trusting her and listening to her when so many others might not have.

When it was all said and done, Larry would have to return to Boston to share his findings with the rest of the legal team, but he assured Valerie he would try his best to make it a quick turnaround. He explained that the department would have to decide whether or not to press charges on Robert Willard posthumously if they considered him guilty; or they could possibly dismiss the matter entirely. If the former, all of the families would be notified that their daughters' deaths would be reclassified as homicides and a court case would ensue. Before he left he released the file room to Valerie, handing her Bill's key ring, and gave his blessing for her to finish cataloging the remainder of the files. He also promised to come back and visit the first moment he could.

Julia called twice after their ill-fated conversation at the café; Valerie neither answered nor returned her calls-- she didn't trust herself not to confront Julia about everything. Barbara on the other hand knew all since Valerie had, against Larry's advisement, told her everything that had transpired, including her date with Larry. It had been years since she had had a close girlfriend to talk with—not since Marian- and it was nice to be able to say out loud to someone who would listen that she missed Larry and looked forward to him visiting. Barbara commiserated with Valerie and continually assured her that everything would work out for the best, including the investigation.

As she waited for word from Boston, Valerie found herself walking the fields behind the campus until she came to the vast expanse of green where the patients were buried. She looked out over the Potter's Field, the stones that marked the patients' graves now covered by the grass that hadn't been tended since the day the asylum had closed. The field was peppered with ankle deep piles of snow that would not be cleared away. Valerie had no idea where Esme's grave actually was though her plot number was noted somewhere in her file; she had no desire to see it. Instead she stood at the edge of the secret cemetery and breathed in the depth of winter, though she was unaware of the cold as she watched one brave woman circling the walking path with a huge golden retriever.

As tired as she was, she found herself wandering toward the community gardens, moving slowly and taking in every detail of the area as if she was preparing to leave forever. In a way she supposed she was, though it wasn't she who would be leaving. It would be the buildings, each brick packed up and taken someplace beyond her reach. Stopping at the edge of the gardens, she looked up beyond the piggery and the garage to the fenced in porches of C Ward, trying to imagine what the hill would look like naked and empty. Of course it wouldn't be that way for long, just long enough to damage the memories. It would be a jarring sight to look at that vast expanse and see nothing but dirt and gravel.

Valerie walked through the maintenance lots and up the hill past the garage. The original Kirkbride plan asylum had been added onto so many times that it was no longer shaped like a bat. It was more like a sprawling square with little U-shaped appendages that twisted in and out of its body like tentacles on an octopus creating hidden courtyards that could only be seen from above. She kept walking towards the back of the wards as dusk descended and the encroaching darkness made the buildings feel as if they were leaning toward her, trying to envelop her. For a brief moment Valerie couldn't help but think she would be alright with that, fitting to be demolished along with the buildings she loved.

Standing outside the wards, Valerie fantasized about walking through the door into another time, a time when the walls swelled with noise and life. But the darker the night became, the harder it was to remember the people who had once made the hospital real. As she turned to walk away, a movement off to the left of the construction fence caught her eye. A shadow stood, mere feet away, watching Valerie as she watched the hospital.

"So you come here too." The woman's voice almost disappeared in the blackness, swept here and there by a light breeze that moved through the cold and reached out its spindly fingers to snatch away her words, but Valerie recognized the voice.

"Hello Julia." She moved closer until she could just make out Julia's face wrapped in a plaid scarf, her hair tucked into a wool hat. "What are you doing here?"

"Just visiting the old girl one last time."

Valerie sniffed. Julia had hated this place, had said so herself. What was she doing reminiscing in the dark? "I think we have some time before this beast comes crashing to the ground," Valerie said coldly.

Julia laughed an odd, forced sort of laugh. "It doesn't matter. Everything else has already come crashing down Val."

"What do you mean?"

Julia closed the distance between them, so close that Valerie could see her breath when she spoke. "You Valerie. You sent everything into a tailspin.""

"What are you talking about Julia?" Valerie pulled her coat tight to her body not because she was cold but because Julia's wild eyes were making her nervous.

Julia kicked at a rock with the toe of her boot and Valerie heard it ping off of the chain link. "If only you hadn't been so high and mighty, so quick to protect my husband's reputation, none of this would have happened."

Valerie stiffened. "What is that supposed to mean?"

"It means," Julia scoffed. "That you were meant to go and tell everyone who would listen that Robert had hit me, how he abused me." She was nearly spitting she was so angry. "You were the lynch pin."

"You're insane Julia." Valerie turned to leave but Julia's hand shot out and grabbed her arm. "You thought I was upset that you betrayed me to that librarian. No, no. I'm surprised you finally loosened those pious lips of yours."

Valerie spun away from Julia, yanking her arm out of her grasp. "So I was just a pawn, is that it Julia?" Larry's words came rushing back to her as she watched Julia standing there, seething. "Oh my God. He didn't hit you at all, did he? You did it yourself!"

Julia's hand shot out and she slapped Valerie across the face. The rush of air that stuck to her fingertips was so icy that it felt like a thousand nails being driven into Valerie's cheek. "You played right into their hands Valerie Martin. If only you had tattled on Robert when he tried to kill you—because mark my words, he would have- I wouldn't have had to take care of it myself."

"What are you talking about?" Valerie cradled her stinging cheek, itching to give Julia a swat in return.

"You're damned right I gave myself those bruises. I came to you all sad and beaten, figuring you would leap to my defense and save me from the wicked Dr. Willard but you let those other women, those whores who wanted nothing more than to take my place in his bed, talk you into keeping quiet. Not once, but twice!"

"You can't be serious. What is wrong with you?"

"Wrong with me? Valerie, the only thing wrong with me is that I didn't have the nerve to kill him sooner."

Valerie's mouth flopped open in disbelief. "Kill him?" She took another step backward, away from Julia, as it dawned on her what she had just admitted to. "Did you kill your husband Julia?"

"Ex-husband Valerie. I finally got up the strength to divorce him remember? I ruined him first though, oh did I ruin him. Bit by bit. And with no help from you I might add." Julia lunged at Valerie, hands out, reaching for her throat. Valerie sidestepped Julia and stuck out her foot, tripping her and letting her fall face first into the grass.

"What are you talking about? Are you insane?" Val watched as Julia rolled over, her chest heaving with the effort to breathe, as she stared up at the night sky. Stars were just starting to appear and illuminate the tears streaming down her cheeks.

Julia threw back her head and laughed. "That man made my life a living hell. He got everything he deserved my friend, and then some."

"Everything? Julia, what did you do?"

Her grin widened in the dark like a hunter locking eyes with its prey. "I took everything that ever mattered to that man-- his whores, those filthy patients, his precious promotions. I drove that Moody girl away. Did you know that?" Of course Valerie had not known that. Lorraine had left without much fanfare but they had all assumed it had been because of shame, not because she had been chased away by the doctor's wife. "I told her that if she didn't leave I would drag her so deep into the mud that she would need a steam shovel to find her way back out."

Valerie couldn't believe what she was hearing. Julia was confessing to dismantling her husband's life, all because he had cheated on her, stepped outside of a marriage that for him was a sham. Then Valerie registered the rest of what Julia had said. "What do you mean 'those filthy patients of his'?"

"All he cared about were those poor excuses for human filth and wretchedness." Julia's tears had dried, her words with them. "None of them deserved his time or his compassion. They were lunatics for Christ's sake!"

"Are you saying…"

"I'm saying I killed Esme. I killed them all!" She shouted, pulling her knees to her chest and beginning to sob again, her hair tangled with the sticks and pebbles that littered the ground. Her coat had come open and her scarf was unwound. She looked like a wild animal.

Valerie sunk down on the ground next to her and stared into the distance. "Say it again."

Julia rolled her head towards Valerie. "What?"

"Say it again. I want to hear you say it again."

Julia sighed heavily and dropped her hands to her chest, eyes to the sky. "I killed Esme. I killed them all."

Valerie didn't say anything, couldn't say anything. She sat next to Julia and simply stared into the dark that was now so black now she couldn't even make out the outlines of the buildings though the weak light of the twinkling stars, so out of place in the wake of such a confession, glinted off the diamond-shaped eyes in the fences. It was as if Valerie was getting a glimpse of what the hill would be like without any buildings.

Julia drew in a massive breath, held it for a moment, then let it out slowly. "And Robert," she said with a whisper. "I killed Robert. I killed him and hoped it would look like he was the one who killed all those girls." She fell silent for a few moments as a million questions bulldozed through Valerie's head but she couldn't find the words to ask any of them.

"I hated him Val," Julia said so quietly that Valerie wasn't sure she had begun to speak again. "I hated him for everything he did to me. He took me away from my family and stole from me the best years of my life when I should have been raising children in a real home. I always wanted children Val, did you know that?"

Another thing Valerie hadn't known. She shook her head though she doubted Julia could see her.

"But he said that an asylum was no place to raise a child. He just didn't want children with me, the woman he had 'taken on' as a favor to his father's old friend, my father. He went to work each day and bonded with the women on the ward in a way that I could never hope he would at home, with me." Her ranting began to pick up speed and she went on and on about the girls, so many girls. She knew what Robert said about her, how he made her out to be some sort of war starved orphan who needed a strong man in her life, all to gain sympathy and usher them into his bed. Julia had wanted a real marriage, a family. "Every night he left me alone to check on his patients or to be with one of those ward girls, I knew. I knew I had to get out."

"Those women—the patients and the ward girls- were human beings. Not just pawns in your nightmare of a marriage."

"Don't you think I know that?" She sat up suddenly, facing Valerie, her hands thrown out to the sky like a lunatic. "Of course I know that but it he deserved it, don't you see? I got rid of them all the only way I knew how."

The words continued to pour from Julia, the words she had held inside for so long, and the torrent was unending. She ranted about her husband putting these strange women with their strange mental diseases on a higher pedestal than her, his own wife. He never treated her as an equal, never even asked her opinion on anything. The only time he had allowed her to take the helm was when they had moved into the cottage and he encouraged her to throw herself into the important task of decorating their "home", a house that she absolutely loathed. Julia hated entertaining the other doctors and their wives. Small talk made her ill and Robert's glad handing, his obvious pursuit of a promotion, made her want to slap him.

Valerie sat and let the woman pour out her soul, every last dark little bit. Julia told her of her return to the ward a few days after Esme was put in restraints. She had taken a bottle of secobarbital from the medicine closet, then returned to the ward. Mrs. Korsinsky was not on duty that night and being a doctor's wife, no one stopped Julia or questioned her. Esme was lying in her bed, groggy from being sedated. Julia crept into her room and undid the restraints so she could make the child sit up, then forced half the bottle of secobarbital down her throat. She waited as the drug took its full effect, then stripped the sheets from Esme's bed and body. Tying them together, she stood on a chair and slung the ribbon of cotton over the light fixture, testing its weight with both hands.

By now tears were streaming down Valerie's cheeks. "You left that child, alone, hanging from her light fixture, without a second thought." Val could barely force her voice above a whisper. "Then you did it again, and again."

"She was so light, like a little bird. I knew no one would question a suicide. You have to understand, it was the only way."

"The only way to what?" Valerie asked, but there was no adequate explanation for Julia's behavior that would ever justify what she had done. "It didn't fix your marriage. It didn't make him a better man. You didn't even succeed in truly ruining him! No one else ever suspected that there was more to those deaths."

"I know that now," Julia huffed, indignantly. "But at the time, I thought it was the only solution."

"And in the end, you killed Robert anyway."

"I just wanted to drag him down, make him understand how it felt to live in that horrid little cottage on this horror of a hill and not have any hope for the future." She shrugged, sending up little puffs of frost; the temperature was dropping and the ground was beginning to turn white with crystallized bits of dew. "It almost worked."

Julia had learned through the grapevine that not long after their divorce Robert had taken up with yet another ward girl. This time he intended to move her into the cottage; he had been passed over for the promotion he so desperately wanted and he no longer had anything to lose. That morning he had been coming down the stairs with a newspaper in his hand, reading while he walked, a habit Julia had always scolded him for. She had always told him that one day he would miss a step, fall and break his neck, so she took advantage of his dangerous reading habits climbing the stairs to meet him. She said he looked surprised to see her, almost happy, until she batted the newspaper out of his hand and started yelling at him, accusing him of ruining her life.

Then she told what she had done to his patients, how she had disposed of them so coldly and callously. If only he had seen what he was doing to her, how she was slowly coming unraveled. As it fully dawned on him what his ex-wife was telling him, his shock turned to anger. He yelled at her, told her what a despicable piece of human trash she was, called their marriage a sham and told her he wished he had never clapped eyes on her. Then, ironically, he raised his hand to strike her.

Julia stepped aside to avoid the blow, then grabbed the hand he had struck out with, pulling as hard as she could. Robert, along with his newspaper, tumbled down the stairs. He landed at the bottom with a sickening thud just as a car came gliding up the driveway. She hurried down the stairs and stepped over Robert's broken body, positioning herself over him. As his girlfriend came through the door, Julia was ready with the crocodile tears and a story about not hearing from her ex for so many days, swearing that she had only come because she was worried about him. Later she would tell the authorities that she had found him lying on the floor, already dead. She sobbed and told them she had warned him something like that would happen if he kept reading on the stairs, and now it had!

Robert's new paramour did not suspect a thing. She believed Julia had only come to check on Robert; she too had scolded him about reading on the stairs so no one thought twice about his death being anything other than an accident. Julia arranged the funeral which was attended by Robert's colleagues and he was cremated, his ashes scattered over the Potter's Field at the hospital. Julia told everyone "her Robert" would have wanted to be close to his hospital. Shortly after that, Julia remarried and moved to Florence with her new husband.

"You've kept this to yourself for all these years."

Julia laughed, a strange, strangled sort of laugh that didn't sound right given the circumstances. "Of course. Do you think I wanted to go to prison?"

"Then why are you telling me now?"

"Because the law can't touch me and no one has connected these women's deaths but you and that idiotic librarian."

"I still don't understand why you would tell me all this."

"Because Valerie, now you have to live with the burden of knowing that you could have stopped all of this from happening. You could have saved them all if you had just done your part."

Valerie began to feel the cold that had seeped into her bones as Julia told her morbid tale. She stood and shook the kinks out of her limbs and straightened her coat. "I'm going to the police."

"Tell whomever you like Val. No one will believe you." Julia stood as well, redoing the buttons on her coat and fixing her scarf. "And I will be long gone."

"You're insane Julia. Completely insane."

"And yet, you know I'm right."

CHAPTER 21

When Larry showed up at her door unexpectedly the next morning, Valerie was still wrapped in her robe finishing her third cup of coffee. She had tossed and turned until dawn, then fallen into a fitful sleep until mid-morning. It was nearly 11:00 when she heard Larry call to her from the porch, his knocking having gone unanswered. She stopped to glance at herself in the hall mirror and started at the sight of herself, her hair sticking up at odd angles, dark circles under her eyes. Tying the belt on her robe a bit tighter, she went to the door and let Larry in, allowing him to kiss her on the cheek as he walked past her.

"Good morning." He pulled a hand from behind his back and presented her with a small bouquet of irises. "I had a few things to follow up on so I decided to surprise you." Larry put his hands on her shoulders and pushed her back, holding her at arm's length for inspection. "What's wrong?"

Valerie took the flowers and though she knew full well that irises wouldn't give off much of a scent, brought them to her nose and inhaled; it was a lovely gesture. "They're beautiful." She went to put them in water leaving Larry standing in the living room,.

"This is a cozy little place."

"I was wrong about Robert Willard," she said, carrying the flowers into the living room and setting them on the coffee table.

Larry stood quietly for a minute, then brought his hand to his forehead as he screwed his eyes shut. "What do you mean you were wrong?"

Valerie walked into the living room and looked out the window across to the abandoned campus. "He didn't kill those women."

"Now is not the time to doubt yourself Valerie."

She shook her head. "I'm not doubting anything Larry. Those women were murdered; just not by Robert Willard."

"Who then?"

"His ex-wife." Valerie turned from the window and smiled sadly at Larry. "You were right about her. She's a manipulative shrew."

"How do you know?" Larry sank onto the couch and leaned back, pinching the bridge of his nose as if to stave off a headache.

Valerie took a seat on the opposite end of the sofa and told him everything that had happened the night before. "She seems to think nothing can happen to her now, not this many years later."

Larry was silent, staring at his hands spread out in his lap. Valerie waited for him to take it all in, then asked, "What do I do now?"

"You tell Bill so that he's in the loop, and then we go to the police."

"Can they do anything after all this time?"

He shrugged. "There's only one way to find out. I'll head over to Haskell and call my bosses, tell them to stop whatever they've got in motion on Willard. You get dressed and meet me over there so we can tell Bill."

Valerie nodded, running her hands through her hair. "I'll go get cleaned up." They both stood and she walked Larry to the door where he kissed her on the forehead again.

"It's going to be fine. We just have to get to the police so they can find Julia Willard." Larry stepped out onto the porch and turned to call over his shoulder. "And for God's sake, make sure your doors are locked."

Valerie watched Larry jog down the stairs and climb into his rental car. She locked the door behind him and went back to the kitchen to make yet another cup of tea, then ran herself a shower. Under the hot spray Valerie closed her eyes and again dreamed of the wards filled with sun slanting vibrantly across the tiled floors. She followed the hallways from one ward to the other, then down into the tunnels. Working shampoo into her hair, she walked the hallways and porches of the Memorial Complex on the other side of the street where the windows stretched down to her knees and she could see down the sweep of the hill to the laundry.

As she rinsed the soap from her skin, the images of the hospital began to fray at the edges, the bright colors dimming under a layer of dirt and grime. Suddenly she was seeing not the hospital of her memories but the ruins that haunted the top of Hospital Hill. She opened her eyes and they stung as little rivulets of soapy water dropped from her lashes. The images of the crumbled wards and shattered walls disintegrated and she was left with a cold fear, a sinking feeling that the hospital's ultimate destruction—figuratively and literally- was nipping at her heels.

She climbed out of the shower and wrapped herself in her robe. In her bedroom she pulled open the curtains, throwing a burst of light into the room and she screamed when she realized there was someone else in her bedroom. Julia Willard was folded neatly into the tiny arm chair next to Valerie's bureau.

"Good morning Val," she said, then glanced down at her watch. "Or should I say afternoon. Tough time sleeping last night?"

"What the hell are you doing in my apartment? How did you get in here?"

Julia cocked her head and regarded Valerie with a half-smile on her face that didn't quite seem to reach her eyes. "Does that really matter Val? I'm sitting in your bedroom, in the dark. What difference does it make how I got here?" Her smile widened into a sneer and she chuckled, shaking her head at Valerie's obvious unease. "You know, I thought a lot last night, about our little chat that we had up at the hospital. So nostalgic, don't you think?"

Julia looked up, waiting for Valerie to answer her, but she had no intention of indulging her in this bizarre line of conversation. She pulled her robe tighter, trying to figure out where she had left her slippers in case she had the opportunity to flee the room but unfortunately the arm chair Julia occupied cut Valerie off from her only means of escape.

"Well I certainly thought it held a sort of…romance, if you will. Not in the traditional sense of course, but there was something satisfying about confessing all my sins right there on the grounds of the hospital that ruined my life."

Valerie scoffed and shook her wet hair away from her face. "It wasn't the hospital that ruined your life Julia. You did it to yourself."

Julia's chin snapped up and she glared at Valerie with a naked hatred that burned itself into Valerie's skin. "If we had just gone and lived in the country like I begged Robert to when we were first married none of this would have happened. I begged him to consider becoming a private physician somewhere in the Berkshires but would he listen? No. Asylum medicine, he said, was the way of the future. Asylum medicine would make him famous because what could he possibly do to distinguish himself as a mere country doctor in the middle of nowhere?"

As Julia ranted Valerie looked over at her bedroom window and wondered if she had remembered to lock it the night before and even though there was no fire escape and they were on the second floor, she wondered if she could make a break for it. The look in Julia's eyes was sending chills up and down Valerie's spine but tried her best to look as if Julia had her undivided attention.

"As I was saying, I was thinking about everything I told you last night." Julia moved her hands in her lap and Valerie realized for the first time that she was holding something and it looked a lot like the base to one of the heavy glass lamps from her night stand. She stole a glance to her left and sure enough one of the lamps was missing, the shade lying on its side on the floor. "I know we used to be close and I could tell you anything, but now that I've thought about it I no longer consider you a friend, especially after you chose that librarian as your little sleuthing partner. By the way, Barbara said to say hello. I paid her a visit this morning."

Valerie's eyes widened. "What did you do Julia?"

"Oh don't worry. I just made sure she knew how unhappy I was about the two of you sniffing around. But I also realize I should have done the same with you, because I'm sure you've blabbed to someone other than Barbara by now."

"I haven't told anyone anything Julia."

Julia shook her head sadly and smiled. "Oh Val, I saw that man leave this morning, the one in the suit. Did you really think I snuck in here without watching your house for a bit first?"

"I didn't tell him a thing Julia. I realized you were right and that there was nothing they could do to you. What would be the point in telling him everything?"

Julia stood, the lamp hanging at her side, the cord dragging across the hardwood floor as she moved closer to the bed. "Part of me is inclined to believe you. I mean, you didn't say a word when my husband nearly strangled you, but that was because you thought you were protecting me. You really have no reason to protect me now that you know what I've done."

"But I also have no reason to expose you Julia." Valerie edged closer to the window and could see that the window was not only off the latch but it was also open a crack. She had gotten up in the middle of the night and needed air; thankfully she hadn't closed it.

"How can I be certain of that Val? How do I know you don't hate me now for what I did to those women you loved so much?" Julia took another half step forward, closing the distance between them ever so slightly more. Her voice had taken on an unsettling sing-song tone that made Valerie's skin crawl. "And let me ask you something that has weighed on me for years—how on earth could you bring yourself to care so deeply about those women? Those broken, shattered, wastes of human space."

Valerie narrowed her eyes and felt a torrent of emotion gather in the back of her throat ready to spring, but then Julia brandished the lamp and continued her rant.

"I never understood why you and Robert encouraged those people. They were never going to get well. They were never going to get their lives back. What a waste of time." Julia turned to stare thoughtfully out the window, the same window that Valerie was hoping to make a break for, that she was slowly inching towards as Julia fell apart right in front of her. "Why would you do it? Why would you give them false hope? I'm the one who did the right thing for those women. I ended their misery." Julia had turned her attention back to Valerie but she didn't seem to notice that Valerie was almost sideways in her bed. "I gave them a chance at life without pain, without their illness. That's more than can be said about the rest of you."

Valerie badly wanted to shout at her, reach out and slap her. Caring for the mentally ill wasn't about ending their suffering like some angel of death, it was about teaching them how to live with what ailed them, how to conquer the demons inside their minds with medication and therapy, then go back out into the world. Valerie never deluded herself thinking that they would be able to return to the lives they used to know because mental illness changed a person in ways that could never be undone, even by the greatest psychiatrist in the world, but at the very least the patients could return to their families, their husbands, their children and make a go of it. There was no reason for them to die, but Valerie wasn't about to argue that point with Julia, not while she was brandishing nearly ten pounds of solid glass.

"I guess that makes me the hero Val, not you. I saved those women. And I saved Robert. I saved him from the stares, the whispers, the rumors. I did what was right."

"The only thing you saved him from was discovering what a monster his ex-wife was." With that Valerie threw up the window, startling Julia so badly that she lost her grip on the lamp and it crashed to the floor, a large piece shattering off the side. Valerie dangled her right leg over the sill and grabbed hold of the window frame, carefully taking her weight off her left foot. Julia retrieved the lamp from the floor and raised it above her head with both hands, charging at Valerie who was hanging from the sill. She tried to pull her left leg all the way out as her right toes dug painfully into the siding but Julia had closed the distance between them, bringing the broken lamp base crashing down onto Valerie's knee.

"You crazy woman!" Valerie reached out and slapped at Julia, the lamp raised above her head, getting ready to strike again. Pain radiated up Valerie's thigh and into her stomach, making her woozy as she tried to maintain her grip on the window frame. Julia brought the lamp down again just as Valerie slid her leg most of the way out, but it wasn't far enough to avoid the second crushing blow that landed on her ankle, slamming it between the lamp base and the window. She lost her grip on the sill as stars bloomed behind her eyes and she felt herself begin to lose consciousness. The last thing she remembered before blacking out was the sensation of floating from the window, the grass and snow below her, and the hospital in the distance.

CHAPTER 22

Larry had gone straight from Valerie's house to the Haskell Building, ready to break the news to Bill about Julia Willard's confession, but it seemed he was late to the party. Bill was at his desk, while Barbara sat on the couch looking visibly shaken.

Bill saw the questioning look on Larry's face and nodded in Barbara's direction. "Julia Willard paid her a visit this morning." He sat forward and rested his elbows on his desk looking imploringly at Larry; he looked like he had no idea how to handle Barbara.

"What happened?" Larry sat down next to her on the couch and put his hand on hers to stop them from shaking.

"She told me everything," Barbara whispered, tears gathering in her eyes. "Then she told me if I went to anyone with the information she would find out and I would regret it."

Bill sat forward, his brows knitted, and splayed his hands out on his desk. "What everything?"

Larry turned to Bill and sighed. "Last night Julia Willard cornered Val up at the hospital." Larry recounted Valerie's conversation with Julia in as much detail as he could. "She told Val she killed the patients and her ex-husband."

"Where is Valerie now?" Bill stood up and was already headed for the door.

"I left her to get dressed. I wanted to fill you in so we could go to the police."

Barbara grabbed Larry's hand and squeezed until he yelped. "You left her alone?"

Seeing the fear in Barbara's eyes, Larry jumped up from the couch and ran after Bill who was already in the lobby and heading for the door. Rather than waste time climbing into one or the other of their cars, they ran across the parking lot, slipping and sliding across the asphalt on their way to Chapel Street. Larry pushed Bill aside and knocked violently on Valerie's door, yelling her name but there was no answer.

"Move out of the way." Larry backed up, then charged the door, planting his shoulder squarely in the middle. The door may have been solid but thankfully the lock was cheap from having been replaced each time a tenant moved out. The door flew open, hitting the wall behind it with a crack that echoed through the empty living room. Larry flew through the apartment looking left and right, realizing that Valerie was nowhere to be found.

"Larry, up here!" Bill had slipped past him and upstairs to the bedroom, surveying the chaos that had been left behind. The covers had been pulled from the bed, the mattress askew on its box spring. The shade from one of the night stand lamps was on the floor, half crushed, and a chair was tipped over near the foot of the bed. Cold air rushed in through the open window, blowing the curtains straight out into the room and drawing both men to the window. "She went out the window," Bill whispered.

Larry turned and ran back downstairs, out to the little patch of ice encrusted grass at the side of the house where he found a discarded, broken lamp base and the dirty gray snow was tinged red with blood. Bill skidded to a stop at Larry's side and looked down at the same grisly tableau, then turned away and threw up in the hedgerow that crowded the foundation behind them.

"We need to call 911. Valerie's gone."

CHAPTER 23

Valerie sat, her back against the cinderblock wall of the tunnel, her legs stretched out in front of her. Her left knee throbbed and her ankle burned with a pain that convinced her that something was likely broken; her entire leg had swelled to twice its normal size. She could also feel blood drying on the back of her head, matting her hair to her skull and she knew it was quite a bit of blood because she had felt it dripping steadily down the back of her neck since the moment she had regain consciousness to find Julia had half-dragging, half frog marching her out to a station wagon that was parked around the corner. Julia hefted Valerie into the back seat and drove her over to the hospital, leaving her half-conscious in front of the fence while she presumably stashed the car. Inside Old Main Julia had draped Valerie's arm across her shoulders and dragged her down the stairs into the tunnels, then to the hallway that led to the morgue.

When Valerie finally opened her eyes Julia stood in the doorway, her back to the morgue, staring at a garish pink hippo in a tutu that had been painted on the wall. "I never did understand why the patients would want to walk past the morgue in order to get to the gym down here. Personally I would have passed on rec time if it meant traipsing by my dead compatriots each time."

Valerie could barely hear her through the pain that sliced through her brain when she opened her eyes so she elected to keep them closed instead. Valerie couldn't have mustered a response to Julia's ravings at that moment if she had tried but Julia didn't seem to care. She began to pace as she spoke, her hands jammed into the pockets of her coat, her breath a phosphorescent white cloud that billowed out before her, then sucked her in as she paced through it.

"Sometimes I can't believe that it will all end here, in this snake pit. But then again, everything I ever dreamed died the moment Robert and I moved here. I think I was happy at least a little while, though I can't really remember anymore. I could just be imagining things." She paused to reach out and touch the frozen stone wall that was ice cold yet somehow still wet with subterranean moisture that seemed to seep from the very ground around them. "We lived on the wards for a time you know. There were suites on one end of the first floor for the doctors who were important, yet not important enough to merit a home away from the lunatics they served."

Valerie remembered seeing those suites once. They were beautiful, opulent almost, designed in the early days when the hospital was only supposed to house 250 patients in comfortable circumstances.. The state hospital was one of the first buildings in town to have steam heat, gas lighting, and indoor plumbing, every room with a view of the grounds.

"I hated being surrounded by those people, literally surrounded on all sides. They did our washing, they cleaned our suite. I hated the thought of them touching my things but Robert said it was necessary for their recovery. What a joke."

Valerie was barely listening to Julia. Instead she sat, wondering if she had any kind of a plan or if she was just going to continue to spiral out of control right there in the tunnels. Somewhere in her subconscious Valerie had accepted that Julia would most likely kill her-- after all she had made the effort to drag her all the way here, to the tunnels where no one would hear her cry out for help, and here she was, talking about it all coming to an end here in the hospital. Did she intend to end it for herself as well?

Julia sighed and slid to the floor across from Valerie, her legs stretched out, almost toe to toe with her. "It was never supposed to be this way." She had started to shiver and tears were slowly rolling down her cheeks. "You and I could have been such great friends Val, under different circumstances of course."

Leaning her head back against the wall, Julia closed her eyes. Watching her carefully as if she was a dangerous animal taking a cat nap, Valerie flexed her toes, testing the pain level that emanated from her limbs—it was excruciating but she felt that if she just tried she could stand up, but she wasn't sure what she would do once she was on her feet. She needed a reason for Julia to help her up and gain her balance, for her to get close enough for Valerie to overtake her somehow.

"Julia, I need to use the bathroom."

At first there was no response, as if she hadn't heard Valerie speak. Then she sighed as if Valerie was getting on her nerves and admitted, "I don't know where it is down here," she said, wiping her nose on the back of her hand.

"It's just down the hall but I can't get up on my own."

Julia sighed and opened her eyes, then pushed herself to her feet. "Alright, alright. Let's go." She bent and looped her arm around Valerie's back, lifting her up slowly onto her one good foot. It took forever for the pair to hobble down the hall but they finally made it to the bathroom and Valerie eased herself through the door. She watched as the door swung shut with her captor on the other side of it; she just had to figure out what to do next.

Looking around, Valerie realized her only way out of this situation was the single window that was high above her head and would require her to climb up on one of the sinks in order to reach it and even then that wasn't a guarantee that she would be able to pull herself up and out. Would she have enough time, she wondered? Testing the stability of the sink closest to the wall, Valerie leaned heavily on it, trying not to flinch when the metal brackets holding up the porcelain bowl creaked and shifted under her. She waited for the wrought iron to settle then leaned forward until her feet lifted off the ground and she was able to ease her right knee onto the edge of the bowl. It felt as if it was taking an eternity to haul herself onto the sink when in reality it was probably only a few minutes. Valerie started to sweat as she slowly pulled her injured left leg up as well, biting her lip against the lightning strike that radiated through her bones and into her chest, threatening to rip her lungs apart.

"Hurry up in there!" Julia banged on the bathroom door, spurring Valerie into action. She put a hand in each corner of the window and pushed until it tilted out, but it was so beaten by the elements and by age that it wouldn't open all the way. Hopefully it would be just enough for Valerie to slip through and she planted her palms on the sill, hauling herself up and sticking her head out the window into the night air. She took a moment to take a good long breath of cold and dark, then transferred her weight to her chest, letting her legs dangle against the inside wall of the bathroom. The pain was unbearable but Valerie pushed on, dragging her lower half up and out the window just as the bathroom door burst open, Julia running into the tiny room in time to see Valerie's feet disappearing out the window. As soon as she was safe she turned over and kicked the window shut with her right foot, then used her elbows to drag her body across the frozen grass.

In her head, Valerie imagined Julia running blindly through the tunnels, searching for the right stairwell that would take her to the surface. Valerie looked around her and realized she had come out just beyond the collapse in Old Main which meant that Julia could choose one of two routes: if she had gone right out of the bathroom she would have to run all the way down to the other side of Old Main in order to get out which would give Valerie a healthy head start. However, if she had gone left, she had only a short distance to go before finding her way to the surface and possibly an open door. Valerie began to pull herself towards the fountain where she would be able to hide from Julia long enough to make her think she had gotten away. Even though it was still daylight they were on the side of the Kirkbride that had the most shelter from the main road; the chances of a passing motorist seeing Valerie this far back were slim to none.

Creeping toward the dense brush that surrounded the fountain, Valerie's arms began to shake with the strain of dragging herself over the chunks of brick and wood that littered the ground around the fountain. For a brief moment Valerie considered falling to the ground and just allowing Julia to find her but adrenaline crowded her veins and spurred her on. The only way any of this would be set right would be to have Julia behind bars, and the only way for that to happen would be for someone to discover Valerie, beaten and bruised, fearing for her life. Taking a deep breath, Valerie pushed on, plowing headlong into the grass and rolling down the tiny hill and into the drainage ditch at the base of the fountain. She let the grasses settle back in around her and closed her eyes, hoping she was hidden well enough, but too exhausted to raise her head to check.

As she lay there, Valerie wondered how it was that everything had spun so far out of control so quickly. Had it only been mere days since Larry had assured her that they had gotten the right man? If she had known this was how it would all come undone she never would have left Westborough. She suddenly found herself missing the comfort and safety of the asylum they fondly called Westie, the one that only knew the "grown up" professional Valerie and held nothing but pleasant, innocuous memories of patients who stayed no longer than a month or two and who she never bonded with. She knew it wasn't normal, the way she had closed herself off to everyone when she moved out to Westborough but it had been the best way she knew to keep the demons at bay. Disconnect, keep to herself.

Making connections and opening herself up to others had only brought pain, death, and fear. If she was honest with herself, she had been afraid of Robert Willard. Yes, she had held her own with him when confronted, but behind that bravado was a healthy dose of terror. The man had been unpredictable, and in some cases Valerie knew that was what had made him attractive to so many women, but she had sensed that there was some instability behind that smooth talking exterior. And though in the end he didn't actually murder those women, he had still be a dangerous man with a volatile temper and a quick hand. After being party to his short fuse and violent reactions, Valerie could not say for certain that he wouldn't have gone on to become a killer. If Julia hadn't stepped in and killed those women there was no telling what Robert Willard might have been capable of. In spite of years of claiming that he and Julia weren't a true match, in the end Robert married a woman who was better suited to him than he could ever have imagined.

"Oh Valerie! Where are you?" Julia's voice wafted over Valerie's hiding place, startling her out of her wits. She sucked air and held her breath, hoping to make herself as small as possible amongst the vines and weeds. "Are you still out here my little wounded bird?" Julia's demented nursery rhyme voice carried through the trees and down the hill but no one else was there to hear her calling wildly for her old friend.

Valerie listened for footfalls, Julia drawing nearer to her hiding place with each step and if she turned her head ever so slightly she was able to see through a part in the overgrowth. Julia was skipping along blithely, bending down every few feet to glance under trees or around piles of rubble. She was coming unraveled and if she found Valerie, she knew this would, without a doubt, be the end.

"Oh Val, why are you hiding from me? I'm your friend." Julia continued to pace ever closer to Valerie's hiding place but it didn't seem that Julia knew she was there. "Valerie! Get out here!" Her voice suddenly turned angry and Julia stamped her feet in the dirt like a petulant child but Valerie stayed perfectly still and deathly quiet.

Julia walked the tree line until she came to the end of the chain link fence around the wards, then trudged back toward the fountain like a lioness pacing in a cage. She was making another pass when Valerie heard voices coming from the direction of the potting shed and Julia must have heard them too because she gasped and took off running.

"Hey! Stop! Julia Willard! Stop where you are!" Valerie recognized that voice. It was Larry's voice and she could now hear his footsteps heading straight for her. Then she heard other voices shouting, other men, and more footsteps running by. Had Larry brought a mob with him? Valerie pushed herself up onto her elbow and peered out of the grass in time to see a small herd of uniformed men in pursuit of Julia Willard-- he had called the police.

"Larry!" Valerie's voice was weak and rough with exhaustion and pain but if she couldn't get Larry's attention now, no one would find her hiding place and she would freeze to death. "Larry! I'm here!" She tried to pull herself up the incline, grabbing onto the base of the fountain but the wrought iron and peeling paint were difficult to hold onto and her hands kept slipping. Putting her head down, her cheek nearly touching the cold, packed dirt below her, Valerie exhaled, resigned to her circumstances.

She must have blacked out right there, curled around the fountain because it was no longer cold. She was back inside the hospital once again, walking slowly through the wards as nurses hurried by her and patients sat idly in the day rooms. Even though there were scores of people around her, not one of them made a sound. Valerie's dream or hallucination or whatever it was, rolled by like a silent film. She began to wonder, was this her heaven? Had she crossed over into an eternal asylum, but one where she would be punished by never being allowed to hear the voices of the people around her? Val wandered through the hospital, the walls freshly painted and cleaned, the floors shining and bright, but no matter how far she walked the hallways seemed never to end, yet she couldn't stop walking.

"Valerie..." She looked up to see a patient approaching her, a girl with flowing raven hair and creamy skin.

"Esme." Val whispered the child's name, reaching out to touch her, but she couldn't seem to get close enough.

"Valerie, wake up."

Was Esme finally speaking to her? Certainly if this was heaven, Esme would be the only one to speak to her after a lifetime of keeping silent. The specter's lips weren't moving but someone was talking to her.

"Valerie, are you still with us?"

Someone was gently shaking her shoulder, saying her name but Valerie resisted, holding on to the image of Esme standing in front of her, still alive and well, but the voice persisted.

"Val. Wake up."

She moaned and shook her head but it was no use. The image of Esme and of the hospital began to fade replaced by the frosted fluorescence of overhead lights that burst into her consciousness. She opened her eyes slowly, looking around her at the wires and tubes, the beeping machines and hissing television that flickered with static.

"Hey sunshine." Someone leaned into her field of vision, Larry. "Nice to have you back." He was holding her hand and he gently squeezed her fingers as her eyes focused on him.

"What happened?"

Larry settled himself on the edge of the bed and tucked Valerie's hand into his lap, rubbing circles on her palm with his thumb. "Julia Willard happened."

Val laughed, then immediately regretted it. Everything hurt, even her ears, and laughing was not a pleasant experience. "I remember some of it. She was in my apartment."

"Yeah we figured that out. Unfortunately we were a few steps behind you."

"How did you find me?"

"I went to see Bill and Barbara was there. Julia had showed up at her apartment that morning and threatened her. We assumed she would do the same with your so we took off for your house by but by the time Bill and I got to your apartment you were already gone."

"She pushed me out the window." Valerie leaned back into the mountain of pillows stacked behind her head and closed her eyes. "She hit me with the lamp and pushed me out the window. Then she dragged me into the hospital. I didn't know what she was going to do with me, I wasn't about to stick around and find out."

"How did you get away from her?"

"I climbed out the bathroom window."

Larry burst out laughing. "You climbed out the bathroom window? With a broken ankle?"

"It's broken?" Val tried to sit up but dizziness washed over her like a wave and she had to sit back.

"Yes it's broken. As are a few of your ribs. You've got a concussion, some nasty cuts and bruises, and your knee is pretty roughed up. Thankfully though everything will heal."

"What about Julia?"

"They're still looking for her."

So she had gotten away for a second time. "Do they have any leads?"

"They tracked her into the woods behind the hospital. They brought dogs and everything, but they lost her scent somewhere near the railroad tracks. The police figure she hopped a train, but I have a hard time believing that."

Valerie nodded. "Same here. Julia isn't the train hopping type. She's still nearby."

"Well, if she tries to come here she'll be in for quite a surprise. There are cops stationed just about everywhere in the hospital. She won't get far."

"Let's hope not."

CHAPTER 24

Two weeks later Valerie was released from the hospital. Larry picked her up in yet another crap rental car and brought her back to her apartment, looping her arm around his shoulders and carrying her carefully up the porch and into the living room, settling her on the couch. Bouncing around her apartment, Larry collected everything he thought Valerie might need to keep her occupied while she recuperated. He tucked pillows behind her back and stacked books on the coffee table which he repositioned so she could reach it. He assembled a tray full of crackers and cheese that she knew had not been in her kitchen before; he must have gone shopping for her at some point. By the time he was done she was wrapped cozily in blankets with a book on her lap and a cup of tea in her hand.

While she read, Larry went around the apartment, dusting and straightening up. When she was done with her tea he washed her cup and put in the drainer to dry. At 4:30 he pulled a roasting chicken out of the refrigerator and started her oven.

"Are you cooking?"

Larry lined a pan with tinfoil and seasoned the chicken, dropping pats of butter onto the skin. "No, I'm knitting a blanket. Of course I'm cooking. You need to eat don't you?"

Valerie laughed. "Didn't you see all the frozen dinners in there?"

"I did but I didn't think you actually ate those!" Larry pretended to look horrified by the thought of her eating microwave meals.

"Of course I eat those. I'm not going to cook full meals just for myself."

"Well then thank God I'm here because man cannot live on freeze dried food alone."

He continued to pull things out of the refrigerator, trimming asparagus and peeling potatoes until an hour later he put a plate in front of Valerie that was heaped with mashed potatoes, buttery asparagus spears, and chicken with a crispy, golden skin.

"This is incredible Larry. I can't believe you can cook like this."

"One of us has to be able to cook otherwise neither of us will survive!"

"Oh is that the case? You plan to make certain I survive, do you?"

Sitting down on the end of the couch, Larry carefully settled himself with Valerie's feet in his lap, keeping her injured ankle elevated. "Yes, I do plan on sticking around to make certain you survive. In fact there's something I wanted to talk to you about." He took a forkful of chicken and put it in his mouth, chewing thoughtfully. "I was thinking it might be good if I stayed out this way for a while."

"Just for a while? Then what? Don't you have to go back to work?" Valerie balanced her plate on her lap and looked at Larry, suddenly horrified by the idea of him going back to Boston.

"Actually, I've requested a transfer."

"Really?"

Larry nodded, his eyes glued firmly to his food. "Yes. Really. In fact it was made official two days ago. I now have an office on the second floor of Haskell."

Valerie tried to hide her smile as she pictured Larry moving into his new office, arranging books, filing away papers. "Where are you going to live?"

"Well..." Larry looked up sheepishly and Valerie knew immediately what he was going to say.

"Yes."

"But I didn't say anything yet."

"You don't have to. Yes. Whatever it is you're going to suggest, yes."

The two looked at each other for a moment, then burst out laughing. It was as if they had been sitting on that couch with each other like that for years, as if time had never passed and it was good. Valerie had never allowed someone to reach her that way but with Larry she just knew it was right and it was safe. There was no reason for her to keep her defenses up the way she had for so many years; it was time to put Robert Willard behind her and let Esme go. If her hallucination while in the hospital had shown her anything, it was that there was nothing left for her in her memories and Esme would have wanted Valerie to have a full and happy life. She couldn't dwell on the past any longer-- she had to move forward and Larry would be there to hold her hand.

"I was thinking we should look at a house or two." Larry was grinning from ear to ear like a kid with a new toy. "The lease on this cottage expires when you finish the filing job, so I was thinking we should look for a house instead."

"You look as if you already have one in mind Mr. Porter."

Larry's grin, already as wide as a Cheshire cat's, spread even wider. "That I do Miss Martin. That I do. But we won't go look at it until you're healed."

Valerie cocked her head and frowned. "But don't we run the risk of it being gone by then? If it's as perfect as you say…"

"Don't worry. It will be there."

Valerie had no idea what kind of black magic Larry possessed that made him so certain about this house but she decided to let it go. He obviously had something up his sleeve and his enthusiasm was contagious.

For the next few weeks Larry took care of Valerie every day, checking in at the office for no more than an hour a day. He also kept tabs on the search for Julia Willard; so far she hadn't surfaced but Larry didn't seem worried. As far as he was concerned, Julia was long gone and wasn't coming back. Valerie didn't necessarily agree but was so focused on her recovery that Julia had become the least of her cares, though there were moments when she would stop and look out the window, wondering just how close she was, but those moments were few and far between.

Then one day the call came—Julia had been apprehended somewhere in Vermont. She had driven her battered station wagon north and managed to talk her way into a job and a room at a roadside motel in the middle of nowhere where no one bothered to check references. Someone staying in the motel recognized Julia from the all-points bulletin the Northampton Police had circulated. She was apprehended while cleaning a guest's room where they found her pocketing cash and jewelry.

Larry had taken the call and though he was in the other room and talking as quietly as he could, Valerie had known that it was Bill who had called and that Julia had been found. She watched him nod and rub his eyes as Bill filled him in on the other end of the line, then hung up and sighed heavily. "They're bringing her back to Northampton and they're going to hold her. She won't get bail, not after what she did to you."

Valerie just nodded, not sure she trusted her voice at that moment. It was a relief but at the same time it made it all real. Julia Willard was now officially a criminal in the eyes of the law, and soon the world would know that she was also a murderer. She doubted there was anything they could charge her with in that regard, but she had certainly made quite an attempt on Valerie's life.

"There will be a trial I'm sure but we'll cross that bridge when we get to it." Larry reached out and hugged Valerie, then kissed her on the forehead. "What do you think of all this?"

What could she think? Julia had been arrested. Arrested! And in a matter of months the hospital would be demolished. The magnitude of it all hit Valerie like a ton of bricks and she burst into tears, crying for all the years she had lost at Northampton State Hospital, for the patients who had lived and died under her watch, and for Robert and Julia Willard whose ruined psyches had so distorted the lives of those around them. Larry held her close and rubbed her back, saying nothing, just holding her as she cried.

"I don't think I can finish."

"Finish what?" Larry pulled back so he could wipe the tears from Valerie's cheeks as she spoke. "Finish the filing work?"

Valerie nodded.

"Oh sweetheart, Bill and I assigned that task weeks ago. In fact it's almost complete now."

Valerie laughed through her tears, dragging the back of her hand across her runny nose. "You mean to tell me that if I had just stuck to the plan and kept my mouth shut I could have been done by now?"

Larry laughed with her, his shoulders shaking and his eyes tearing up. "Now, what fun would that have been?"

EPILOGUE

Val stood at the base of Hospital Hill and watched as scores of people milled around, some already looking up expectantly, others chatting quietly while they waited. Larry was up front, talking with some of the event organizers, helping to keep the morning on track as much as possible while the wind whipped around everyone's heads. It was mid-November, a mere week away from Thanksgiving, and it was already bitterly cold; in fact Valerie was surprised so many people had come out for the event. The sky, clear and gray, threatened to open up at the slightest provocation but somehow that felt just right to her.

Larry joined her, nudging her gently in the side and leaning in to speak quietly as everyone else seemed to be doing. "Someone said there are over 1,000 people here."

Valerie looked around at the crowd that had grown substantially while she had been staring up the hill. People of all ages had gathered around her, many with children in tow as senior citizens stood shoulder to shoulder with teenagers who carried cameras around their necks. It was certainly quite a group. "It's amazing," she breathed.

It was almost time, time to take a last walk up that steep hill to the front of Old Main, past the fountain that had finally been cleared of all the brush and brambles that had saved Valerie's life; past the potter's shed and right up to the fence line that snaked its way around the gothic giant of an asylum.

"Valerie Martin. As I live and breathe."

Valerie turned, expecting to see Barbara Graham, or maybe even Bill's secretary Margie, but instead she stood face to face with a woman who looked a lot like someone she hadn't seen in more than thirty years.

"Marian?" Valerie felt a lump at the back of her throat as the woman smiled her familiar crooked smile and stepped forward with outstretched arms.

"How the hell are you Val?" She said, hugging her old friend as tight as she dared, then holding her at arm's length so she could look at her. "You haven't changed a bit!"

"Neither have you! You look as if you haven't aged a day since 1980!"

"Nonsense. I look old. I feel old." Marian shook her head. "Hell, I am old!"

Valerie snorted. "We both are my friend. My God. What are you doing here?"

Marian jerked a thumb in Larry's direction and grinned. "This one over here. Apparently he waits until you're safely asleep and then snoops through your things."

Turning to Larry, Valerie let her mouth fall open in disbelief. "Is that true Mr. Porter?"

A wave of crimson guilt crept up Larry's neck and reddened his ears. "You caught me. I went through your photo albums from when you were here and

212

Marian was in almost every single picture so I took the liberty of tracking her down."

"He wrote to me and lucky for him I inherited the farm when my parents passed. As soon as I got his letter I packed up the car and headed east. I wouldn't have missed this for the world."

The crowd in front of them was beginning to move, slowly ascending the hill to Old Main. Looping her arm through Valerie's, Marian took her first steps toward the hospital in over thirty years. On Valerie's other side, Larry slide his hand into hers and the three of them followed the crowd. It was almost noon when they reached the top and they stood, the tattered curtains flapping in the now open windows. All of the windows in the Kirkbride had been flung open, just for today, just for this moment and it looked as if the hospital could finally breathe.

Just moments before noon the skies opened up and a light hail fell, bouncing off the red brick, clattering to the ground but no one moved except to brush the tiny stones off their shoulders. Suddenly there was a hint of a sound, the beginnings of a joyful chorus of music that began to drift from the empty windows of the asylum. Those standing in front of the building were silent, some barely breathing, as the opening bars of Bach's Magnificat poured over them and wound its way through the trees, over the rooftops, and down the hill. There were hundreds of speakers inside the hospital pumping out a joyful tribute to the thousands of souls within the stone walls, until after seven minutes, the sun broke through the clouds and bathed the hilltop in warmth.

Valerie turned her face to the sun and closed her eyes, imagining the music pouring from the windows carrying the spirits of the dead out into the light.

Marian leaned in and whispered in Valerie's ear. "Esme would have loved this."

She squeezed Marian's arm and felt the tears welling in her eyes. She was right, Esme would have loved it. When it was over, the crowd milled around for a bit but slowly, ever so slowly, everyone dispersed, returning to their houses and their gardens, their lives that would, someday soon, no longer include the hospital. Walking away from the hospital that day, Valerie knew it would be the last time she would visit Hospital Hill even though she and Larry hadn't moved very far. When she was finally recovered Larry took her to see the house he wanted to buy—the farm house that had once belonged to the hospital. They purchased it directly from the department and moved in just before Valerie's birthday in June. Larry was still working out of the Haskell Building but Valerie had decided to finally take retirement and go back to her writing.

As they rounded the corner onto Chapel Street, Valerie took one last look over her shoulder. The building was quiet now and a late afternoon faux winter dusk had settled over the Kirkbride. Valerie nodded, as if to say goodbye to the hospital on the hill, then joined Marian and Larry on the sidewalk where they were discussing how long Marian might stay. It was nice to have her around again, as if she had never left. Valerie fell into step with Marian, Larry falling behind to give the women some time to talk as they headed for the farmhouse where Larry would light a fire in the fireplace and cook dinner while Val and Marian caught up.

In the approaching twilight, the state hospital sat, it too in its twilight time. In a few short years the only sign of the asylum's existence would be just that: a sign. The Village at Hospital Hill would take its place and the rest would disappear, the hill changed forever. Now that Julia Willard was behind bars Valerie believed that Esme and the others would finally be able to rest and the grounds would be exorcised of its demons. Though it made her unspeakably sad to see the hospital in such an advanced state of decay, she realized it was time for it to go.

The Department had offered Valerie the opportunity to aid in notifying the girls' families but she declined. She had enough to carry with her that she did not want the burden of hearing the voices of their loved ones for the rest of her life. Instead she enjoyed her time with Marian, promising to write to her often and planning a visit to her farm in New York to meet her husband and children. Soon after Larry took her out to the garden behind their farmhouse and asked her to marry him. She said yes without hesitation; in the end the people in her life were the only memories she wanted from Northampton State Hospital.

Valerie did go back to Hospital Hill once more, the day they demolished Old Main. She watched from the fence line as a bucket loader swung its monstrous arm through the brick, reducing it to a pile of shattered brick and concrete, then they collapsed the tunnels where Julia had held Valerie captive and filled them in with dirt. As the bulldozer pushed the rubble into a pile in the middle of the now empty field in front of her old dorm, Valerie turned away, then looked over her shoulder one last time and imagined she saw every memory of the asylum disappear into the clouds like a genie released from a bottle.

AUTHOR'S NOTE

This novel is, first and foremost, a work of fiction. While Northampton State Hospital and the Haskell Building are real, Valerie and her compatriots are not, nor are the patients and staff members represented in this book. Bits and pieces of the Northampton State Hospital historical timeline have been altered to suit Valerie's time at the hospital and certain facts and figures have been changed in order to better fit the story.

Northampton State Hospital was constructed in 1856 and was the third of its kind in Massachusetts, joining Worcester State Hospital and Danvers State Hospital in the east. From the air, the asylum looks like a bat with its wings outstretched—the Kirkbride Plan- and the wards were arranged such that the least involved patients were housed closest to the center administration building and the most violent at the tips of the wings with men and women separated. The asylum had its own bowling alley, theater, and beauty salon. In the early days the patients worked the farm and cared for the pigs, bees, and dairy herd.

By the late 1950's when Valerie would have been working at Northampton, the hospital was beginning to fall into disrepair and was painfully overcrowded. With the advent of psychiatric medications, coma treatments, and hydrotherapy, the care of the insane began to change and the state of Massachusetts began to move towards deinstitutionalization.

The grand portico that Valerie walks through on the day of her interview, collapsed and was demolished in 1986. All that remained was the front façade and the wrought iron fountain that saves Valerie from Julia at the end of the novel. The fountain is now in storage awaiting restoration and its return to the Northampton State Hospital Memorial Park upon its completion.

Demolition of Old Main was completed in 2006 to make way for new development on Hospital Hill followed by the Memorial Complex the next summer. The Haskell Building is the last remaining, operating Department of Mental Health program on the former state hospital campus.

ACKNOWLEDGEMENTS

First and foremost, a great deal of thanks to Tom Riddell at Smith College and his History of Northampton State Hospital class. Thanks to the efforts of his students, the Northampton State Hospital Memorial Park will be a reality in the near future.

Thanks to Brenda Rusch for being the first set of eyes on Hospital Hill when it was but a bare bones first draft, and to Liz Rasczka for being the final set of eyes and being an unforgiving line editor!

I also owe a great deal to those who have taken the time to read and respond to my work: Justin Taylor for patiently workshopping Hospital Hill and helping me get to know Valerie better; Megan Granger who has been an unflagging writing partner throughout the last semester; and Greg Meuse, a patient sounding board for a few terrible editing ideas that led to many great ones.

For all my fellow readers and writers on the WriteOn website and all those who have voted for Hospital Hill during my Kindle Scout Campaign, thank you for your unending support!

28463184R00124

Made in the USA
Middletown, DE
16 January 2016